Prologue

Ellie hugs her knees to her breasts, and then stretches out languidly, before recoiling into a foetal position once again. Her bed is not broad, only a narrow truckle bed placed against the wall of her small room, but she still moves her slim frame around it freely as the dream invades her sleep, disturbing her peace — deeply.

It is always the same scenario. She, as a small child, lying on a soft feather bed, a large bed with sheets so smooth they slip over her young body as a swan glides onto an ice covered lake in winter. Only this bed is warm, and soft, and her fair curls fall loosely over the pillow. Pale green eyes are shielded from the world by closed lids. Ellie's senses live the dreams, craving more, as if she were really that child. The sensation of a silk nightgown against

1

her young skin, beautifully smooth, makes a sleepy smile cross the woman's face. The child clings to the feel of the soft, clean warmth as her head rests on a white linen pillowcase edged with silk ribbon, over a soft down filled cushion. The details of the sumptuous surroundings are as clear to Ellie as the finely decorated small bird appliquéd on the corner of her pillow. Ellie lost in the feeling of joy, slumbers on.

Then, as it always does, the whole ambiance changes: large hands tear her from her image of a childhood heaven. The young girl screams and fights, still clinging to that precious pillow, but the bird is ripped from her hands and is flung onto the floor: a carpeted floor, rich burgundy in colour, it lands next to a pair of small cream silk slippers, the same little bird embroidered upon each one.

The villains wrap her in a cloak. Ellie feels the child's panic, as she listens to strange muffled voices inaudibly whispered around her. She hears a name being called in the distance, but it is not hers, too long, too faint to fully discern the words clearly. Unceremoniously, she is carried by a strong arm as the man runs down stairs with her as his bundle. Screaming in her cloaked cocoon, the child is taken out into the night air.

It all seems so real. The child cries for her mother and receives a slap. A shout goes up and she is thrown abruptly onto the floor of a waiting carriage, the fall so abrupt that Ellie jumps at the force, as if it was she who had been tossed back into her cot. She sits bolt upright on her hard bed. With perspiration moistening her brow, despite the cold of the night in her single blanket and the fireless room, reality has returned.

Ellie stands and shakes her head; her fair curls hang free over her shoulders. She has had this dream before. It always occurs in winter, always toying with her senses, giving the same mixture of emotions: the warmth of a cosy bed and then the cold as she is ripped from it. Her nightmare ends as she is left bereft and alone.

This time is no different. She awoke to find herself a woman grown, having a fanciful dream, which somehow she never manages to conclude. This time the effect is more urgent, more disturbing, her senses refusing to allow her to return to her sleep.

Ellie wraps her blanket around her shoulders, not wanting to go back to her cot for the few precious hours of sleep that could be left to her before her day should begin. Ellie slips out of her room, the attic room, to the window on the landing which leads to the main stairs. The dark mahogany stairs lead down to the family bedchambers — her aunt's and her two cousins'. Below them are the day rooms, the dining room and gallery, the library, and a study. Beneath these the busiest places exist in white-washed corridors and rooms: the sculleries, the laundry, the stores, kitchen, and dairy rooms and, behind the hall, the stable block and coach house. Here is where the servants toil. Ellie is also too familiar with them, because they are also her domain.

Ellie stares at the moon through the window before opening it. She needs to breathe fresh air. Despite the chill of the night, Ellie has to bring her senses back to her life here, her reality, and away from fanciful dreams and notions of an existence beyond her own. With no thought of reason, impulsively she needs to feel the night air on her skin — to feel alive and free. Carefully, she steps out onto the lower part of the roof under the window, onto a ledge, and walks delicately to the corner of the building. Here she leans back against the cold tiles of the sloping roof and stares at the stars, wondering if anyone else is watching them this night, or if she alone admires them. Should she make a wish like a child? She breathes in, filling her lungs with the fresh night air. What would she wish for? Her parents — why make an impossible wish? Ellie could not feel their nearness in her spirit. It is as though their images had been wiped from her mind. She must have seen them in her young life, but try as she might she cannot bring an image to mind, the memory of a tender touch or the whisper of a loving word.

She thinks again and smiles. 'Love!' She folds her arms across her body below her breasts and hugs herself. 'I wish for . . . I pray, God forgive me,' but despite knowing she should be praying for an end to war and suffering, and for peace — one word sums up her heart's desire — 'love!' Besides, she reasons, if the world generally could love more, wars would not exist. She smiles at the notion, a single star twinkles back at her. For a few moments she allows her blanket to fall to her sides. The air pinches her skin through her thin cotton nightgown. It is a world removed from her dream, and one that brings reality back to her, filling her senses and clearing her mind. With one glance back at her favourite star, she turns and leaves her special place, retracing her steps to the boundaries of the house.

Ellie desires so much more than she has, yet, she does not know what or why. She has been given a home out of the charity of her distant family and has much to be grateful for. Her own family's shame is not attached to her; they have been blanked from the world — only she is testimony that they ever existed, but her aunt has taken great strides to keep the stigma of her mother's reckless actions from her. Yet, Ellie resents it, being beholden to these people, living under the shame which is none of her doing, so she dreams. Her ingratitude has to remain hidden from her Aunt Gertrude, but when this dream returns, the feeling wells up within her and she has to feel free, feel the air around her, breathing in and out, in her own special space.

Before returning to the window she looks around, admiring the grounds of this fine manor house, seeing shapes of animals move as the moon lights up all below it. Up here she feels detached from the toil, the monotony of the existence she has to endure within the hall's walls. A movement catches her eye at the edge of the woods: perhaps a deer. She peers down into the night; the reflection is on something light, a face staring upwards. No, no animal looks so, as this form stands on two legs. For the first time since she discovered this special place she feels anxious. Ellie has no fear of height or of nature, but humans, they make her nervous. At least, strangers do, and if she was watching him . . . could he be watching her?

The stranger seems to be staring up at the hall. Ellie wraps her blanket tightly around her and, with stealth, tiptoes back to the window. She climbs in silently, never glancing down or back, because she must not be seen; her secret place must stay hers. Whoever he is, he risks being caught by the game-keeper and that is something she would not wish on anyone, for the magistrate owns a large estate nearby and takes no pity on those who steal off his land, even if their families hunger.

Making sure the window is secured she returns to her small attic room and nestles onto her hard bed, pulls her lumpy pillow under her head and tries to go back to sleep. For a few precious moments after being exposed to the night air, her little room feels almost warm. In this short time she will descend into a dreamless sleep until the sun rises, when Rosie, the oldest of the housemaids, will wake her and Ellie's new day will begin.

1

Ellie entered the morning room carrying her aunt's tray. As Gertrude's companion she had a mixed role, one between a distant relative and personal maid. Her existence depended upon the whim of the very dour Mrs Gertrude Hemming, widow of the late Mr Archibald Hemming, a second son of a once wealthy family, who owned land in the south. Unfortunately for Gertrude, fortunes can change with the turn of a card — a bad one, and a fortune can be lost. Her uncle's untimely death left his widow with debts, so she and their daughters only had enough funds left to retire to this, their manor house in the northern reaches of the county of Yorkshire. A remote and heartless place, Gertrude often bemoaned, but to Ellie it was wild and beautiful, rich in nature. Despite the poverty within the county, Gertrude could only feel her own suffering at the loss of a life within southern society, and the gaiety of London.

'Ellie, my dear, place that tray down on the table and come and sit by me. I have something I want to tell you.' Her aunt patted the tapestry covered sofa next to her with her lace-gloved hand.

Ellie was quite surprised by her aunt's familiar tone. This was not how she normally addressed her. Usually, particularly on a morning, a wave of a hand sufficed to dismiss her, the tray would be left and Ellie would go to the kitchens and discuss the day's menus, make sure the linens were in order, depending upon which day of the week it was, and then deal with any problems the servants may have encountered.

'Is there something, wrong, Aunt?' Ellie asked, as she sat on the edge of the sofa next to the brown haired lady, who always wore a silver grey, laced, cap. She insisted it complemented her 'natural' hair colour. Ellie knew that her greying hair was combed with tea every night and morning, which gave it its brown colour, although the hue was known to vary from day to day.

'Why should there be anything wrong, Ellie?' Her aunt almost smiled at her, then she noticed that one of Ellie's wayward curls had escaped from its place. 'Girl, you are really going to have to pay more attention to that hair of yours. If you were seen in polite society with such a wanton look, people would talk. They may even hazard guesses as to your origins . . . and we do not want that!' Her normal manner slipped through the pleasant façade.

Ellie blushed slightly. The reference to her mother hurt her deeply. She knew that her mother had run away when she was small. It was said she went off with an officer — a French officer from 'Les bleus' the name given to the new guard in the early days of the Revolutionary Wars. It was said she was not a 'lady' and got what she deserved, but no one ever told her what that was. A lot had been said on the matter as it was regularly referred to by her aunt, whom she totally depended on for her keep. However, in public Gertrude had always presented Ellie as the daughter of her brother, a war hero, who had died leaving an unfortunate, orphaned child. Ellie was therefore forced to acknowledge how much Gertrude protected her from the wrath of society, should the truth have been known. Ellie watched her as Gertrude posed again ready to divulge the information she had for her.

'See to it later, girl. Now, I have some excellent news for you. You are in your twentieth year and obviously can not spend your days frittering away time around here.' Again, there was an unusual — almost compassionate look in Gertrude's eyes. Unusual and some-what disconcerting, thought Ellie.

Ellie smiled; she dreamed of going to London to see the city. To have the opportunity to do what her cousins had, and 'come out' in their society. She had seen their dresses, shoes, jewellery, and longed to go with them. However, it had not been allowed as she had been told she was needed to stay and look after the hall. They had both been betrothed within a month of each other and now they waited to marry in the coming spring. Ellie just wanted to see the sights, go beyond the estate — and live. Her eyes widened in open expectation, pale green jewels in a face surrounded by her golden curls. Ellie had no notion of how beautiful a woman she had turned into. She had never been allowed to have a looking glass in her bedroom as her aunt forbade such vanity — after all, Gertrude had said to her, it had been the downfall of Ellie's mother, lest she should forget.

'You are to come out. You are a little older than would be ideal and your nature is not as genteel as perhaps it should be, I know, but putting your shortcomings aside you have enough of my dear brother's attributes and breeding to make you a viable bride, so you are still to come out. Admittedly, you are gangly and are of dubious birth, but we have sorted all that out. It will not be a problem for you, I have made arrangements and you shall meet your betrothed at a Christmas ball.' Her aunt's mouth set into that firm line. She had said what she wanted to and now waited for Ellie's submissive nod.

'A ball, in London?' she said, softly. 'Am I to go to London for the season?'

The doors to the morning room opened and Cybil and Esme entered. Her cousins were dressed in fine muslin day gowns: one in apple green, the other in primrose yellow, both in stark contrast to their dark hair and strong features. Esme was to marry a captain who was presently serving in Oporto, whilst Esme would become Mrs Hardwick, married to the owner of Hardwick's Cotton Mill and Clothing Emporium — one to old money and one to new. The new seemed to have more than the old in an annual income as his 'empire' grew and sought to buy land adjoining the estate on which they now lived.

'In London!' her aunt repeated. 'Do you think we wish to be a laughing stock of the city? No my girl, if we were to send you out in the city, in no time at all we would be the ridiculed by society. Your bad blood would not stand such fine scrutiny.'

Ellie flushed. She was always hurt and her pride dented when her past was thrown at her in such a manner. It was something she never became used to. She could not help what her parents had done. Yet, it was she who had been left to carry the stigma of her mother's actions. In her heart she only pined to know the woman, and could not, therefore, condemn her, when she had only one viewpoint known to her. Ellie often wondered if her mother had found true love, or been tricked by the foreigner. How they met at all was a complete mystery to her. Could she have been unhappy with her own father? Perhaps the brother was like his sister Gertrude, in which case she could definitely not condemn such a rash act of escapism. Her cheeks flushed, she had condemned her father without knowing him either.

'We had aimed to have the ball in the assembly rooms in Harrogate, but alas,' the woman glanced at her daughters who had seated themselves on the window seats with their embroidery in hand. ' . . . the weather is not right for it . . . '

'You mean I am to come out now? In winter? Not in the spring? What of my clothes, my wardrobe? How will I have time to prepare for such an event by Christmas?' Ellie stood up.

Esme laughed, as Cybil gasped.

'My girl, we have two weddings to prepare for in the spring. Do you really think we can afford to prepare a wardrobe and a full season for you also?' Her aunt shook her head. 'Sometimes your ingratitude shocks me to the core of my soul! I have been blessed with two dear daughters who consider me greatly but you, girl, take take take!'

Ellie swallowed. She knew she had spoken out of turn, knew her dream of silk slippers and the warmth of a feather bed had distorted her mind, given her 'fancy ideas' as Rosie would say. 'I did not think. I apologise for my rash comments.'

'No, you did not and frequently do not. That is my task in life to think for you, until Gerald takes on the chore, and then that will be his challenge and burden in life, from this Christmas onwards, that is.' Her aunt was staring at her, her grey eyes fixed on Ellie's sapphire ones.

Ellie froze. 'Gerald whom?' She realised now that what Gertrude was planning was not a 'coming out' but a match — a marriage to suit her convenience and ends. Ellie felt an inner chill grow inside her. Different to the refreshing night air, this was one of dread, bordering fear. Her life was about to be dictated again. Far from opening up to exciting possibilities, it appeared to be closing in on her again.

'Mr Gerald Cookson, my cousin, on my mother's side and also, as it happens, our family solicitor. He has a practice in Gorebeck, so you will be able to visit here often and still look after your aunt, occasionally, in my dotage.' The false smile revealed browning teeth.

'Now, Mama, you are nowhere near that yet,' remarked Cybil, as Esme nodded in agreement, her mouth full of Cook's freshly baked biscuits and blackberry jam.

'Your cousin . . . ' Ellie repeated, ignoring the other young women.

'You are extremely fortunate, child. He is aware of your circumstances and after due consideration and the moderately recent death of his beloved wife, Amelia, he has decided that it is time he took another, younger one. His discretion can be guaranteed. You have done

19

well to secure such a prospect. He is established and has a lovely town house. His youngest son will soon be sent to St Austin's Boarding School over at Middlebeck. So you will have space for your own children in his house when I do not require you to visit here. You are much younger and stronger than Amelia was, poor thing, she so wanted that baby girl. Still, not to ponder — one woman's loss is another's gain.'

She winked at Ellie, as Ellie felt her stomach knot. She was to replace a woman who had died in childbirth.

'But I have never met the man, Aunt Gertrude,' Ellie faltered, as she caught the disapproving glint in Esme's eye. 'What if we are not comfortable with each other? How old is he? How will we have anything in common? I know nothing of the law.' Ellie's voice had risen slightly, triggering a look of disapproval from her aunt.

'Heavens above! No, you do not nor should you need to. He is a man matured. You have been blessed with good fortune. He has a house in Harrogate, a farm nearby and is said to be thinking of buying another office there. Can you imagine, all that property and the man has other business interests overseas? And you . . . well your past shall be buried and never mentioned again, as well it should be. He already has two sons so you have no pressure on you there. You have no need to worry, child. He will not reject you, I have given him good references as to your abilities at running a home, instructing domestics and that you are of pleasant appearance and manners. He is content with that. We will have the ball just before Christmas and you shall be married in our own little chapel in the New Year. His family is small; he has a mother who normally resides in his home in Harrogate. I understand she moved back in with him when Amelia left him all alone. However, once you are established as his wife, he will have her moved back. A man needs a wife — not a mother to fuss over him. I am sure she will also approve of you.' She looked at Ellie and smiled, showing her uneven discoloured teeth, a sight usually hidden from the world by a stiff pair of lips.

Ellie could see the woman was really pleased with her plans.

'Now, you have no need to thank me yet; there will be ample time for that over the future years when you can count your blessings, girl. Think on it, he will not be gallivanting around Europe getting himself shot at like the younger men.' She raised her hand to stop a protest from Cybil at her tactless words, as Esme gasped in horror as she obviously thought about her gallant Captain. 'Believe me, girl, there are advantages to not having the demands of a younger husband. Just go about your business and we shall talk again of it. Then I shall show you the dress pattern I have selected for your ball gown — nothing too frivolous, Gerald has a reputation to uphold. He cannot be seen with a young flibbertigibbet of a wife who does not know how to behave in mature company. Your wedding dress will be a simple affair, as he will expect a sober wife and not one given to whims or frippery. You must curb that wayward spirit and learn to make your husband content. See how your aunt cares for you, and me with my own daughters' needs to see to, yet I still have put your needs first.' She looked at her daughters who smiled appreciatively back at her.

Ellie backed away, her stomach so tight it ached, her head screaming like the child in her dream for now she found herself in a living nightmare. She closed the door behind her, but made not for the kitchens to see Cook; instead, she headed out across the cobbled stones of the courtyard, beyond the stables to the woodland. She walked, tripped and stumbled over tree roots, lifting her skirts so that only her boots were muddied, until she came to the river bank that cut this forest land in two.

Standing on a large flat rock which overhung the fast-flowing river she stared down at the moving mass of water. It was free to run its course, unlike Ellie, who watched helpless as tears ran down her fair cheeks. She had no reason to expect anything other than a life as a companion or servant. She lacked even the basic skills needed to be a respected governess, her education had been limited and she was not gifted in any of the skills a woman should be, from embroidery to playing the pianoforte, her aunt was always telling her so. Even if she was offered a life as a governess it would be no more than another lonely life without any prospects of happiness and no one to call upon as a friend. She had been given the chance of something far greater than that — a future, a husband, a position with someone of rank in the community and therefore she would have some authority, a home of her own, and the chance to have a family, raised with a respected name. Yet her heart was breaking. She wanted none of it. She had wished for love only the night before and instead her reward had been to have the futility of her own 'existence' thrown in her face! Ellie felt more alone than ever she had before in her life. To perform a role of wife, housekeeper, step-mother to recently bereaved children and . . . then to become a lover, to a stranger, who sounded old enough to be her father, with no love. Was that what her life would be? To be that of a performing marionette to a stranger to please her aunt's convenience. Her temper, normally so calm and tolerant, raged inside her.

The wind blew at her. Her lack of sleep made her feel lightheaded and a feeling of total despair swept over her. She swayed, mesmerised by the water, her thoughts as mixed and tumultuous as the flow below her. She felt as though she would drift away, invisible to the world, only to be missed for the roles she could no longer fulfil, but never known for being herself, never to be free of Gertrude or wake again . . . Suddenly, she was swept away. Not by the wind, nor the pain caused by the thoughts that dominated her mind, but by a strong pair of arms that encircled her waist, lifting her bodily back off the rock.

Ellie snapped from her maudlin thoughts and started to kick and fight as she was returned to the path. The heel of her boot contacted the leg of her abductor and instantly she was released; dropped, unceremoniously from his grip, as she hit the ground with a thud, falling directly upon her rump.

'Halt! Woman! Do you want to injure me when I have just saved your damned life?' The voice was strong and commanding, the face determined and the manner abrupt.

Ellie was facing a tall man, a gentleman, wearing a Garrick, hat, knee breeches and tall black riding boots, standing over her. He was broad of shoulder, with dark hair, cut to his neck and, annoyingly, Ellie saw that a slight smile played on his well formed lips.

'Saved my life?' Ellie repeated as she gathered her wits, whilst still staring at this stranger. Arranging her skirts, she stood up with as much dignity as she could muster, whilst she wiped the seat of her dress and flicked her hem out. It was then she noticed his horse tethered to a nearby tree. A fine animal, obviously of good stock, like its master, she presumed. She had been so lost in her own dismal thoughts that she had not even heard him ride up on the path behind her.

'Yes, miss, you nearly fell in the river, did you not?' He pointed with his crop to the stone on which she had been standing. 'Or had you a desire to throw yourself into its flow?'

'No, I was just . . . ' Involuntarily, she shivered.

He stepped forward, removing his

caped coat and swung it around her shoulders. 'Here, wear this, woman, or you will freeze to death.' He flicked a curl of blonde hair from her face with his gloved hand. She could smell his cologne, mingled with the odour of horse; he had obviously ridden quite a way. She breathed them in and her head cleared; she was suddenly very alive — thankfully she had not fallen, in a moment of madness, off the stone.

'I was not falling into the river. I was only thinking, not of jumping you understand, it was the wind . . . it was far stronger than I realised . . . I . . . ' Ellie offered her words feebly, as an excuse.

Removing his glove he traced the path of a tear across her cheek with his finger. 'Sad thoughts, I should say, miss.' He looked at her with curiosity showing in his deep brown eyes and she wondered what thoughts of her had crossed behind them as she must have looked a pathetic sight.

Ellie looked down and blushed.

'They were private thoughts, sir. Not worthy of voicing. You must excuse me, I must return to the hall.' She was going to swing his coat from her back. It was so long as it nestled upon her frame that it almost touched the grass beneath her feet.

'No, wear it, I shall walk a way with you, my horse needs a rest from the ride. We may as well talk, and then I can decide whether such sad thoughts are worth voicing when you share them with me.' He smiled warmly at her.

Ellie thought he had a kind face, but worldly. However, her world had become a busy confusing place. 'Why would I tell a stranger the workings of my mind?' she asked.

'Because he saved you from a thorough soaking at least and a drowning in the worst scenario. I will see you safely back to your mistress and you can tell me what it is that saddens you on such a lovely day as this,' he persisted.

At the mention of the word 'mistress' Ellie's pride prickled. 'I would not be as presumptuous of your time, sir.' Ellie swung his coat off her back. She smoothed the cape as she hung it over her arm and offered it back to its owner. The familiarity of wearing a man's garment, still warm from his own back, made her uneasy. Her emotions, already troubled, were in enough turmoil without further distraction. Ellie realised she had life-changing decisions to make, and fast. 'My mistress?' she queried.

'Yes, you work at the hall do you not? Are you not a housemaid?' he replied, hesitating, after replacing his coat and untying the reins of the horse, leading it back to where Ellie stood.

'No, sir, I do not. I am not any sort of maid. I live there with my aunt.' She folded her arms and stared at him, the surprise on his face was clear and, Ellie decided, insulting. She was not a maid, but obviously he had thought her beneath him in every respect. Unfairly, she wondered why he had bothered to 'save' her.

He stopped. Bowed low in an exaggerated gesture of politeness, and then stood up, his eyes meeting hers. 'You must forgive my impudence and presumptions, miss. Let us return to the hall together then and you can have the servants announce me.' He stood straight.

Ellie flushed. He was standing facing her; she had to tilt her head to look up at him, his coat was almost touching her as she stared at him, unmoving.

'I can hardly announce you, sir, as I do not know whom it is I should be announcing. We have hardly been introduced and I can not introduce you to my aunt as the stranger who took liberties with my person, by sweeping me up in his arms!' She smiled politely back at him.

'Saved your life, miss. It sounds more heroic and accurate.' His smile dropped. He leaned forward slightly so that his face was level with hers. 'You may introduce me, miss, and tell them what ever you may wish to about the manner of our meeting. I would not mention anything about taking liberties or I should then have to defend myself by explaining where you were, what you were doing and I hardly think Mrs Gertrude Hemming would approve, do you?' He waited for her to respond but she stared silently looking at him, as there was nothing she could retort with. 'My name is Cookson, miss, Mr Gerald Cookson.

2

Ellie stared at the face looking back into hers. The square jaw line, dark piercing eyes and his confident manner made her swallow involuntarily as she stood her ground, defiantly looking back at this arrogant man. She reasoned he may be as many as ten summers older than her, which was less than she had at first presumed on hearing her aunt's announcement of the match. Perhaps she should have stayed longer and questioned her aunt further instead of scurrying away like a frightened hare. It had been such a shock to her that she was even being considered for marriage.

She wondered if this gentleman, clearly in his prime, could really be her suitor. He was far removed from the image she had formed of him in her mind when her aunt had described him earlier in the day. How quickly, she thought, life can change.

'Are you a man of the law, sir?' she asked quietly.

He looked surprised. 'Indeed I am but I am surprised my successes have been talked about within the hall.'

He folded his arms and watched her as she swallowed and tried to regain her composure. 'If you ride along the road you will shortly arrive at the gates to the hall. I suggest you announce your arrival, sir. Although . . . ' she looked around her at the uneven rutted road as she searched for the right words, wishing he would just go and leave her to sort out her thoughts which had descended into a mess of confusion. 'Good day, sir!' she exclaimed, and made to step away from him, but he took hold of her arm, firmly, without exerting enough force to cause her any pain, but enough to stop her in her tracks.

'You had not finished your sentence, miss. You said, 'Although . . . ' without qualifying what you intended to say. That, after presuming I was intending to go to the hall. Pray, finish your statement, and tell me how you know my intentions before I even do myself?'

She looked down at his hand and then stared into the depth of his eyes. He had confidence bordering outright arrogance. She was determined not to show how intimidated she felt by his patronising manner — by his very presence. She saw a faint smile appear on his lips as he released his grip. He nodded, acknowledging her displeasure, releasing her arm.

'My apologies for being presumptuous miss.'

'I was going to say, sir, that you may be a few months earlier than you were expected, that was all.' She saw a look of bewilderment replace his smile.

'That is fascinating, because as far as I am aware, I am not expected at all. However, I am intrigued to know who this young maid is who apparently is privy to knowledge about my affairs.'

He tilted his head to one side and raised his fingers to his mouth. 'Oh my Lord, you are not a sooth-sayer, are you? Do you possess 'gifts'? If so, my dear, you should keep this to yourself, for I have heard that they still burn witches in this back-water.' He dropped his hand down and laughed at his own sarcastic humour.

'Indeed, why would I be? Surely you have discussed your plans in depth with Aunt Gertrude.'

'Do you?' he answered, thoughtfully. 'What an intriguing creature you are? You speak in riddles.'

'Creature! Good day, sir!' Ellie turned away from him, she had said too much. It was not her position to question a man of property about his viewpoint of the world or his business intentions. She walked briskly towards the narrow path that would take her back through the forest to the side gate in the walled garden of the estate. It was the way she had entered and left the estate since she came to it as a small child. She could hardly remember that time, for she had been very ill when she was first carried into the hall and could not remember the world before it. This, she supposed, was why her mind played cruel tricks upon her by creating the idyllic childhood in her dreams, always to be destroyed by the harshness of her reality. When the stranger had grabbed her, for one awful moment the panic that had awoken the child, which always seemed so real, had been mirrored by her own distress. She had kicked out mercilessly at this stranger — not as the child had but, being a woman full-grown, as a woman her kicks had held far more force. She had just kicked, insulted and been rude to her intended suitor.

She heard his horse gallop away. Which way it travelled she could not tell. Her head wanted him to go away, far away and leave her alone, whilst she somehow managed to compose herself, and attune to the idea of being any man's wife, let alone his. Her spirits seemed more obliged to the idea now, having seen the man. It had been a timely chance meeting. Ellie was surprised. She had asked for love and that notion had been destroyed by Gertrude, but providence had stepped in, and she realised that she did not want him to gallop away without her being able to spend some time with him. What was behind that confident, arrogant manner? He was her future. He was a mystery to her. She stopped and looked back toward the river. Somehow she had to try and undo the image he would have of her in his mind — the sad pathetic 'creature' by a river, and replace it with the image of a healthy, amiable young woman. What would he think of her standing crying like a child upon a rock, nearly falling into the river? She shivered, realising the truth in his words. She had been near to falling and the thought terrified her, for she could not swim and would have been swept to a certain death. How was she to face him again if he turned up at the hall? She had acted as a foolish girl. Her 'intended' was some years older than her, but she had never imagined him to be so athletic of build, fashionable, strong and determined in mind as well as body, with an uncertain humour and an air of authority. In short, she had previously pictured her new life as one of a challenge of endurance. Now, she realised the challenge was of a very different kind — one that she was determined to meet. Ellie would prepare herself so that next time he was presented with a sophisticated young woman. She smiled — well perhaps a well-groomed one and not a little fool.

Ellie paused before entering the garden beyond the gates; he had saved her from fainting and falling into the river. He knew she had been upset. No wonder he thought her to be a housemaid. She put her hand on the iron handle of the gate; her life at the hall was not much better than that of Rosie's anyway. Her existence was about to change. She licked her fingers and tried to control her wayward curls before entering, then wiped her face with her skirt to try to remove all trace of tears, and stood proud and straight. If she was to become a married woman, to such a man, then she would make sure she was equal to the match.

She allowed a smile to cross her face as, inside, some strange feeling was born, not fear or foreboding, but one of excitement and uncertainty. It was new and dangerous, but because of it she suddenly felt alive, as she did when she faced the stars. He would learn to love and respect her, as she would him.

★ ★ ★

Rosie was crossing the front hall when the door was flung open wide. The outline of a fine looking man was silhouetted in the doorway by the autumn sunshine. Gerald entered; the old place had not changed much.

'Good day, sir . . . There is a large

iron lion upon the door, sir, it was put there so that unannounced visitors could knock . . . sir! Do you possess a card as well as a crop, sir, or could you tell me who it is that I say is calling in such a rude manner . . . ' Rosie moved closer. 'Eee, lad, it can't be, after all these years . . . it isn't, is it?' She put down the empty tray on the hall table and rushed forward. Her skirts swishing around her ample figure as she scurried over to greet him. She peered up at the man, squinting and straining; she was not five feet three inches in height and he was near six full feet tall. 'It is, isn't it?'

'Well, young Rosie, as fresh and lovely as your fragrant namesake, it rather depends on who you want 'it' to be?' He bent lower so that she could see his face clearly.

'Oh bless you, sir. This house was a much duller place, for sure, without your young mischief around here, sir. It is young Mr Gerald, isn't it?' She ushered him in, taking his crop, hat and coat. Nearly swamped by the material of his Garrick, he helped her to place it on a peg on the wall to the side of the main doors.

'Yes, Rosie, I have returned for a brief visit to see my favourite maid.' He smiled warmly at her.

'You have words of honey and a mind that is filled with mischief. Favourite maidservant indeed. I bet you have turned the heads of many a young maid, sir, servant or not.' She laughed as he shrugged his shoulders as if unaware of his charms. 'I shall tell madam you are here. It is good to see you again, sir. I have long hoped that you would lay the past to rest and rejoin us for a visit. Don't do to harbour grudges, Mr Gerald.' She blushed. 'I shall see you are announced, ignore my ramblings.'

'I am glad that you still can, Rosie. How long has your sight been failing, Rosie?' He had fond memories of this woman, the only ones he had of this place. She had always brought him cakes and fancies to cheer him up when things brought him low — namely her mistress and her temper. He never could seem to be good enough at anything to please her; to him she was the devil's handmaiden.

Rosie's head shot around. 'Please, sir, don't say anything to them. I can still manage to do my chores, sir. We don't get many strangers around these parts, so everyone's familiar. I know this place like the back of my hand. I couldn't survive in a strange one.'

She had changed; she obviously lived in fear of the day when she could no longer cope. He could see the worry in her.

He patted her shoulder reassuringly. 'Go and tell 'Gertie' that I am here.'

Rosie laughed, 'Eee, sir, you always was a one! 'Gertie' indeed, just as well she can't take a hand to you no more.'

'I would love to see her try,' he answered. There was little humour in his words.

The woman laughed at him and

shook her head as she walked away. 'I am so glad to see you, sir . . . And after such news of your father. I bet you got a real shock, so soon after the loss of Mrs Amelia.' She blushed a little, realising her tongue had run away with her; she quickly continued walking away. 'It won't take a moment, sir. You make yourself at home.'

He followed her to the morning room, waiting outside for the announcement to be made of his presence. He knew that word was slow to travel to and from this part of the northeast but wondered what his cantankerous father had done now. His thoughts, however, were still with the young girl who had been so distressed by the river. Who was she? Why was she so put out? But the one question that disturbed him the most was why she should be so familiar with him, to the point of expecting him to visit this house — a building he had avoided since his unhappy childhood years here. This visit was perhaps long overdue. He also thought of her because no matter what her problem was that had taken her to such a place, she was pretty in face and gentle in manner — unlike Gertrude and her daughters.

3

Rosie knocked on the door and waited a few moments until 'Gertie' decided to answer her.

'What is it now, Rosie?' Rosie entered, leaving the door slightly ajar.

'We have a visitor, ma'am.' Rosie blustered into the room. She was obviously very happy and excited by his sudden, unexpected appearance.

'Here! Today! Unannounced! Who would do such a thing?' Getrude looked to her two daughters who instantly stood up, smoothing out their skirts and checking their hair in the large looking glass by the side of the marble mantelpiece. Esme pinched her cheeks to give them a little colour.

'Mr Gerald Cookson, ma'am,' Rosie announced, trying hard to keep the eagerness and sheer joy from her voice.

'Here?'

Rosie nodded, her white cloth cap flopping around her grey hair which was pinned tightly underneath it. 'Just outside the doors, ma'am,' she whispered, pointing as if Gertrude would not know where her own doors were.

'Well, show him in then, and arrange for some refreshments for our unexpected guest. Warm the green bedroom through and have it made ready for him for he will not travel back tonight of that I am sure. Then you go and tell that lazy good-for-nothing girl to make herself ready to be presented to her future husband. He obviously is keener for this marriage than I had realised.' She turned to Cybil and Esme. 'Girls, I want you to go and find one of your better day dresses for her to wear. Oh! Don't look at me like that; you will have many more made for your trousseau. Now quickly, make her presentable and tell the silly girl to smile pleasantly not like a country bumpkin. I am depending on you both to see to it that she looks at her best; she needs to make a good impression. It is vitally important this marriage goes through as planned. Go!' She stood up and gestured with her hands that they hurry.

Both young women scurried obediently out of the room, whilst Gertrude arranged her skirts sitting back down sedately on the sofa where she had been seated, and wondered why he was bringing their arrangements forward without consulting her first. Had he found something out which was going to change their plans? She hoped not, time was running out and they had planned for this for so long. Gertrude placed her embroidery down on the inlaid cherry wood table in front of her. She smiled pleasantly and waited for her cousin to enter the room. He must have more news for her. They were so near to achieving their dream that it was all she could do to sit still and stay composed. The door moved, she straightened her back and placed her hands upon her lap in a genteel manner. Mr Gerald Cookson was announced by Rosie.

He entered the morning room with an easy gait and his usual air of confidence, as if he owned the building he was in — but not yet, the lease was still held by them, the property owned by his father.

Gertrude gripped the edge of the sofa at either side of her, her face paled. If he inherited it she was sure he would have them placed in the workhouse. She managed to speak only one word, 'You!' before standing and facing her unexpected and unwanted guest.

'My dear, Aunt Gertrude, how pleasant it is to see that you have not changed in these past . . . five, no six years. I trust you are as well and as robust as ever.' He saw her smile disappear the moment he entered the room. She had paled, she was shocked, it was worth this visit just to see her thrown in such a way.

'I am not your aunt, Gerald. I thought you had learned never to call me such. I prefer you to refer to me as madam, as you well know.' She walked over to the window and looked out. 'You are not here with your father then?'

Gerald, feeling the disappointment in her voice looked around him. 'Apparently, it would appear I am not, madam.'

'Your ridiculous wit has not matured in any way. I can see that also. Do you have word of him? Is he ill?"

Gerald looked at her. Genuine concern had entered her expression and voice. She was holding her hands together in front of her. That back of hers, he thought, straight as an arrow and as unyielding as mahogany.

She seemed to be watching him with a strangely intense stare. Something was not right in this hall, and Gerald was feeling a strong need to defer his business and linger a while to find out precisely what it was, and what the girl knew about it.

'He is as well as he ever is. He is still fat in belly, opinionated in mouth and coarse of manner. So, he is as well as he ever will be.' He grinned.

'It is you who are coarse, boy. Along with disrespectful, ungrateful and inconsiderate. I could have been entertaining!' she snapped. Her face flushed at his words. He knew she hated this semi-rural life.

'Were you expecting word from him, madam?' he asked politely, as he sat down on the window seat. He completely ignored her insults, over the years he had heard so many that they no longer held any hurt or bruising for him; boarding school had succeeded in toughening him up in a way she had failed to. Her reproofs seemed irrelevant. She walked over to the large marble fireplace opposite as if not wanting to share his space.

'My cousin is very caring; he always sends word when he can.'

'He did not know I was coming. Father lost his wife, you know. Amelia was a kind soul. I was saddened by this piece of news, because she was one of life's genteel ladies and deserved to have a happy life. After my mother died, he was single for many years, I had been pleased that he had found himself an amicable companion, but it is a shame he did not know how to keep her that way.' He watched her mouth set in a tense line, a look that as a boy would have terrified him, but as a man he saw her for the bitter woman that she was.

'She was weak in character, simple in spirit, and feeble in flesh.' The words poured from Gertie's mouth in a simple, uncontrolled stream of vitriol. 'Gerald deserved a stronger woman, one that could look after him, until his time for eternity came around.' Her eyes showed no emotion; he heard her words of harsh facts.

He knew that she believed totally that her will, her judgement was correct and she would fight and justify her actions to anyone until she had her way.

'Really, your comments do you no service. I see that the milk of human kindness still flows through your veins, madam.' He crossed his legs and leaned back slightly.

'Did you travel here merely to upset me, Gerald? After these years have passed do you still have to take out your grief of your mother's death on your poor caring aunt? You know how I prefer you to be known as Gideon. Your middle name is far more fitting for you. Your father suits Gerald very well. He can carry it with aplomb; there is no point to having two men in a family named the same. It would serve you well in London to be known as Gideon Cookson, and be different — separate to such a noble gentleman as your father. How goes it in the Inns, or have you swapped Lincoln Inn and law for the other kind, a tavern, which may fulfil your preferred pastimes. Do you cater for gentry or are you lodged in Gin Alley, or the Dials?' She stayed by the mantelpiece, not sitting just staring at him, trying to insult, hurt or provoke him in her usual nonchalant manner.

'I am doing very well, madam. I have passed my examinations and now practice in the city. I have established a name — my own.' He saw her disappointment; she had hoped that he would fail, like his father had in the Inns of London, but he had not.

'Then I shall arrange for you to be fed and should hate to keep such an important man from his business any longer than needs be.' She pulled on the bell cord.

'That would be very welcoming of you. I shall eat whilst my room is prepared and then we can speak further of . . . ' his words ceased mid sentence. Ellie had entered the room, dressed in a white muslin day gown and silver slippers. Her hair had been brushed up to sit in curls atop her crown. It was encircled by a single velvet emerald green ribbon, which accentuated the colour of her eyes and contrasted with the golden locks which it held in place. Her cheeks flushed slightly as his eyes quickly took in every detail of her image . . . tantalising him, as he looked upon this vision of classic loveliness.

'Yes, Ellie, what is it girl, what do you want?' Gertrude's colour deepened as did the dark shadow which crossed her eyes.

Ellie would normally have been flustered, but Gerald had stood and now moved over to her. He stared down into her eyes and she smiled.

'I must apologise for my surprise to see you so soon, but I had not expected you to arrive until just before Christmas. The news is still fresh to me, of the betrothal, but I am certain that, in time, we shall . . . ' Ellie felt uncomfortable. Not because of his presence but because of her aunts.

He took her hand in his and kissed the back of it. 'Indeed, Miss Ellie, we shall.' He stood straight, glancing toward Gertrude whose colour had deepened to a shade of puce, eyes darkening with a cloud of displeasure.

Ellie felt the slight squeeze of his

hand against her fingers before he released it.

'What are you talking about, you stupid girl!' Gertrude's voice rose. This time Ellie did take notice as she saw how angry her aunt was.

'Mama . . . ' Cybil began to placate her mother.

'This is Mr Gerald Cookson, is it not?' Ellie asked, confused as to what was happening.

'No!' Gertrude snapped.

Ellie looked at him.

'I am,' he replied, and shrugged, obviously enjoying this moment.

'His son. This is Mr Gerald Cookson's son, girl . . . This is my cousin's son!' She shook a finger in Gerald's direction.

Ellie felt her world cloud over, with the same menacing feeling that had sent her senses in a whirl by the river. She could not speak, think . . . or hope. She felt as a fool. Esme's stifled giggle did not help her embarrassment any.

'Forgive me miss, for not making that

immediately clear to you. It would seem that news of this happy event has crossed with my earlier arrival here. We have both been mistaken. Let us take a walk in the walled garden, where we can discuss your plans, then we can both understand clearly what path lies ahead.' He tried to deflect her situation, taking away their embarrassment and awkwardness as Ellie was clearly shocked.

'You will do no such thing!' Gertrude blustered. Then, after looking at Cybil's disapproving look, as if the daughter was trying to calm the mother's actions if not her actual feelings, Gertrude nodded at her daughter and she stilled as a storm suddenly abates upon the sea. 'I should advise you to take your food and rest, sir. Then, Gerald, you and I shall talk again. Ellie, you shall accompany Cybil and Esme to visit Miss Parkes this afternoon seeing as you are suitably dressed for visiting your betters. Mind you, not a word of your plans must be divulged. The girl is a gossip and this shall be done in an appropriate manner,' she looked up at Gerald, who stood with his arms folded across his chest casually, 'whilst Gerald and I have chance to catch up with many events he has missed after being away for so long. It has been too long.'

'Indeed,' he agreed, 'Miss, we shall talk at dinner.' He made his exit, being collected by Rosie and shown into the dining room.

Gertrude, with mouth and fists clenched, followed on behind him, leaving the young women to enjoy the afternoon together.

Ellie just stared as the vision of her future walked out of the room, to be replaced with the overwhelming aura of despair. He was so handsome, she thought, and then cringed at the thought of marrying his father and looking upon such a fine man as her 'stepson' — it just could not be. Somehow she had to escape and ruin Gertrude's plans for her, without being her own ruin in the process.

4

Ellie found herself seated in a carriage opposite Esme and Cybil. Wearing their bonnets, spencer and gloves, all three contrasted in looks and colour scheme despite each outfit being totally co-ordinated. Ellie was by far the fairest, slimmest, prettiest and delicate in her emerald spencer, which matched her hair band with the trimming on her hat. She was also the most unhappy of the three young women, as she knew it would be beyond them to have any understanding or compassion for how she was feeling. She had rarely had the opportunity to share their presence without Gertrude along as a chaperone. Which meant their sisterly bond did not extend to her.

'Well, Ellie, you poor thing, what a mess that was and what a complete fool you looked, so eager to accept Mr

Cookson's son as your beau. What a totally embarrassing mistake to make — almost desperate!' Esme remarked. It could have been a comforting understanding comment she chose to make; instead her words hurt deeply, for the shard of truth within them cut her.

Ellie swallowed. Her cheeks heightened in colour. She saw the spark in Esme's eyes glow brighter as she had created the menace she yearned for. The woman continued, obviously pleased with the impact her comments were making.

'Thank goodness nothing like that happened when we came out in society last summer. I swear, I would have fainted where I stood. No one would have looked the same side of the street we were on if we had been so bold and awkwardly wrong.' She shook her head with exaggerated dismay and looked to her sister.

'It was an obvious mistake to make, under the circumstances . . . that is if one did not stop to think about the difference in the men's ages,' Cybil countered, looking a little more sombre and thoughtful than her sister had. 'For him to have his own practice is possible, and I suppose two sons if they were but infants, but even so, to look so keen is quite shameful.'

One thing there was no mistaking, thought Ellie, that Cybil was definitely her mother's daughter.

'Think nothing of it, Ellie. Mama, will put all right. There was nobody else there to witness it, other than family and Cookson himself. Surely he would not spread gossip and ruin your reputation in polite circles, before you have chance to do it yourself — I mean establish a reputation, that is.' She smiled, obviously intending to offer insult.

Esme giggled at her sister's deliberate faux pas. Ellie felt a tide of anger rising within her. She was by nature a calm person, who liked to think the best of people, but these two young women and their mother had dented Ellie's faith in human nature — or at least in theirs.

'Mind you, he looked like a cad to me,' Cybil continued. 'I have seen his like before. He will dally with gamblers, drinkers and no doubt . . . unkempt women. We have been out in 'society'; you have not, so we can tell a real gentleman apart from a cad, by his manners and the look in the eye. Eyes give so much away, do they not, Esme?'

Esme nodded her agreement. 'Definitely, windows to the soul! Did you see the way he appeared to rub mother up, and enjoyed doing it, by his arrogant manner? So incorrigible. I should think he would be a difficult man to control. Still, he has a fine physique. I also think he must be approaching his thirtieth year — heading past his prime.' She paused for a thoughtful moment as she glanced out of the coach's small window. 'I wonder how old his father actually is.' Her attention returned to Ellie. 'Perhaps Gerald the younger is already wed or promised. I mean a man such as he will not be short of eligible admirers.' She sighed. 'You must not let him use your embarrassment to tease you when you are his step-mother. You will have to act his superior.'

Ellie stared out of the carriage window, trying to ignore all their words as if they were part of the coach's continuous noise as they traversed the uneven surface of the old road. She stared across the open land to the distant headland. The noise continued, like the turning of the wheels and momentum of the vehicle.

'If the son is such a good looking gentleman, cad or not, I am sure that the father will also be of fine stature — good looking, that is, and not a cad. Oh dear, we do seem to be saying all the unfortunate things.'

Ellie stayed quiet, still gazing at the landscape outside, restraining herself from telling them to be quiet then and save their inane comments for when they were in their own company and could enjoy their little quips on their own. Ellie wished she could escape from the claustrophobic atmosphere inside the carriage, the endless babble, and walk with only her own company, free, over the fields to the coast. She had rarely seen the sea, but had marvelled at its vastness when she had. She closed her eyes for a moment and visualised a warmer climate, fine sand, a gentle slope to a warm ocean. What would it feel like to have water lapping at her bare feet, her naked legs, her . . .

'Ellie!' Esme snapped. Instantly the blissful image in Ellie's mind shattered, her senses numbed to banality once more. 'Have you nothing you wish to say upon the matter of your marriage? We are all to be wed and you will be first. How exciting will that be? We have trousseaus to plan, feasts to agree, and honeymoons to contemplate.' She gripped her sister's hand excitedly. 'I can not wait for that!' she laughed as Cybil gasped. 'We are to go as a four to London first, then to Bath to take the waters and then on to the Lake District before returning via Harrogate Spa. We were going to tour Europe, but alas, Napoleon is still being a nuisance, so we shall tour our own wonderful land instead. It will be such fun.'

Ellie restrained an impulse to laugh, wondering if Lord Wellington thought Napoleon was still being a 'nuisance' also, and if he had interrupted his plans for the summer. Did the man realise that people could no longer set out on a grand tour and that many rich folk had been inconvenienced by the Emperor's desire to rule the continent? Ellie may be naive, but she read news sheets when she could, listened to news brought into the house by traders who supplied the household with goods from Harrogate, York, Whitby and sometimes even Newcastle when the winter coal supply was restocked. She was only too aware of the reality of the situation in the troubled world beyond their shores and the possibility that if all did not go well for their brave soldiers, invasion was another reality they may yet have to face.

'. . . You were to come along with us as our companion, but that will have to change now. Gerald the elder does not wish to travel. I suppose age does slow one down a little. We may have to take Rosie instead.' She looked up in mock despair.

'You are beyond the pale at times, Esme.' Cybil looked to Ellie. 'You are fortunate, Ellie, he is a man of maturity and has worldly experience. I am sure that he will want your companionship more than other . . . exertions.'

Esme chuckled. 'I would rather he exerted himself, but then, I am in love and it will make wifely duties so much more acceptable, or dare I say — enjoyable.'

Cybil blushed and put her hand to her mouth.

'How would you know?' Ellie asked sharply.

'How dare you! Do you infer I have

been less than a lady, Ellie? Your jealous nature does you no credit. It will not help you in your new life. If you do not learn to hold in your feelings, showing only the finer behaviour expected of a young wife, then that jealousy you feel inside will eat up your soul, as you spend every family gathering watching us with our young families, whilst you can only compare your step sons to their father. Especially as one already knows you were more than willing to be matched to him.' She shook her head. Esme folded her hands on her lap, looking directly at Ellie, with a mixture of a challenge and smug contentment in her manner.

'It is the only thing to do, Ellie. Be thankful you will have a good home to look after and the respect in society that marriage to an established, wealthy man, can give you.' Cybil nodded at her, as if to reinforce her words.

Ellie swallowed so to control her frustration and anger. 'I am not jealous of either of you. I wish you every possible happiness as you enter into your wedded idyll. I hope you have many children, healthy and without the many problems that childbirth can combine. Do not worry for me, ladies, for I will make the best of my lot, as I always have done.' She smiled sweetly at their stunned faces. Marriage seemed like the perfect symbol of success to them, but childbirth was another thing altogether. It robbed many a maid of her youth, her looks, and often, of their life.

Esme opened her mouth to rebuke Ellie again, but Cybil raised her hand to still the conversation. 'Let us travel in peace and admire the countryside and ponder our futures. I am sure we will be at Miss Parkes' house soon enough. Remember, though, Mama forbade us to gossip about your marriage, Ellie. You may want to gloat about your own good fortune and the wealth you will marry into, but you must resist the desire to boast as yours has not been announced, yet. Mama is a stickler for propriety.'

Ellie smiled back at them, this time her response was genuine. 'I will say nothing of it and listen as you two delight Miss Parkes, and me, with all the details of your plans. I may learn a lot from you.' They seemed a little bemused by her words as if they were unsure of her sincerity. She was very sincere for she had been told little enough detail about their plans. Ellie had not known that she had been invited as an escort to the young brides on their honeymoon. It was a common enough practice for a bride to take a friend with them to act as a companion to her when her husband was busy elsewhere. She could not imagine being a confidante or support to these two self-absorbed women. However, in all their empty conversation they had said one thing which had brought a smile to Ellie's lips and heart — her marriage had not been announced. Cybil was right; the match was not yet secure. It had not been settled, nor had she agreed to it. Surely she had the final say in it. She had seen the son and had imagined a fine future with such a man — a lifelong challenge and adventure. How could she replace that image in her mind with that of the father, no matter how respectable, wealthy and accomplished he may be? His previous wives had both died; she did not wish to be his third.

She committed her mind for the next three hours to listening to Esme and Cybil bragging in front of the plain, single but wealthy Miss Parkes, who also said little in response. Esme and Cybil seemed not to notice this but, as they rose to leave, the two left the room ahead of Ellie and Miss Parkes as they made their way back toward the waiting coach.

Miss Parkes walked with Ellie. 'I do not envy you, Ellie,' she whispered. 'They are quite insufferable, even for a few hours company.'

Ellie almost laughed, but controlled her need to let out a display of genuine emotions, so instead smiled widely. 'That I can not say, Miss Parkes.'

'I know you can not, which is why I have. When they have left you all alone with their domineering and equally dull mama, to venture into wedded bliss, you must come and visit me on your own. I should like to know you better.' She patted Ellie's arm.

'Do you not wish to be married, Miss Parkes?' Ellie had asked her new friend openly before she gave the words thought as to their impropriety.

'Never! Why should I share my mother's wealth with some money grabbing spoilt man child. No, Ellie, if I have a man in my life, it will be on my own terms.' She looked at Ellie. 'Do I shock you?'

'No, but I envy you not your wealth, but the freedom it has given you,' Ellie replied.

'Then content yourself with the knowledge and wisdom of my future plight, as those two will have you believe that my lack of a suitor will mean that I will die a lonely old maid. You can visit me in my dotage and share some of my loneliness. They do not see that I am pestered by opportunists with ill fortune, gamblers who have wasted their wealth and those who are just filled with greed for more. If I can find one genuine heart I would indeed be happy. Until then I shall enjoy what I have to the fullest that I am able.'

'Ellie!' Esme's voice shouted back to them.

'Coming,' Ellie replied. 'I shall look forward to seeing you again. Thank you.' The last two words brought a smile and a gesture that they should hasten to the coach, where Cybil and Esme were seating themselves, obviously anxious that they should not be left out of any conversation.

'Thank you, Miss Parkes, do be sure to call on us soon. Mama always enjoys your company.' Cybil waved as they departed, Miss Parkes nodded as if agreeing she would — one day.

'I hope you learned something about how ladies conduct themselves in polite society,' Esme commented. 'What was she saying as you left there?'

'She was commenting on how you are both so happy about your futures, and hopes that you will be happy.' She looked earnestly from one to the other.

Esme seemed content with this explanation. 'Did you see her eyes widen when I told her that my fiancé is currently choosing our new coach?' She looked from Cybil to Ellie. 'The news also impressed me greatly, at first, but one has to learn to cover up one's feelings and accept these things as normal, because in a very short time new coaches, gowns and a life of assemblies and gaiety will be my new 'normality'.'

'You made a very strong impression upon her, of that I am certain, Esme.' Ellie saw her straighten her back with pride.

'I do not need you to tell me that, dear. One knows.' She smiled at Cybil who nodded at her in agreement, but who then looked straight at Ellie, her smile dropping to be replaced by a thinly veiled look of warning.

★ ★ ★

'So, Aunt Gertrude, what pot of brew do you stir now? Why is my father agreeing to marry such a young girl? Where have you been hiding her? I have not heard talk of 'Ellie' before.' Gerald sipped the glass of wine; he felt warm, comfortable and had let his guard down as he relaxed.

'Gideon, dear . . . ' Gertrude began to speak in a honeyed voice. 'I am not your aunt.'

'Gerald, madam,' he corrected.

'Gerald, you are a man full grown. Surely you can see why a mature lonely gentleman would want to find himself a healthy young wife to see him into his dotage.' She had regained some composure and sank into a more commodious manner of speech. 'Who knows, you may even have another brother by this time next year. Then you would have even more reason to succeed in your own right. You are the eldest and as such the family will ultimately depend upon you. She is fit, and I think will make your father an amiable companion where the other two failed. You should not insult me. I am not surprised you know nothing of Ellie for you hardly ever return to this part of the country — your home. Or has your success in the city made you look down on your humbler roots?'

'Yes, I can see why Father may want a younger wife — eventually, but why this particular one? She is young, pretty and totally wrong for the mature man you refer to, who seemed quite content with his harridan of a house keeper, his mama and his visits to his club. Where did you find her?' Gerald watched her; there was something in her manner which unsettled him. She had always been close to his father, which was why she had been entrusted to raise his son from a young child, when his wife died of a bout of a simple cold which unexpectedly had turned fatal.

'When did you last see him, boy?' Gertrude watched him as he sat eating his food which had been laid out for him in the dining room.

'Why don't you join me, woman?' he asked.

'I have eaten,' she replied. 'Do not call me a 'woman'; you will remember your manners!'

'Then sit with me and let us talk, madam. We have not engaged in any meaningful conversation, Aunt, for many years. Let us start afresh, time is a great healer and I appreciate that on my last visit I may have spoken out of turn.' He smiled at her remembering her puce face when he accused her of being a witch.

'Time has distorted your memory, for you were beyond vulgar, ungrateful, arrogant, disrespectful, and loathsome and . . .'

'Would it help if I apologised to you,

sincerely; I was young, grieving and often provoked. Esme has a way with words that leaves an impression upon a man . . . or should I say boy. I hear she is to wed also.'

'Esme speaks her mind as you clearly do. She would have made a suitable match for you. However, I accept your apologies and never expect you to be so disrespectful when you visit me in my home again, sir. Remember I am also of an age with your father. You will not abuse me so freely, sir.' She took a deep intake of breath to fill her lungs, her ample bosom rising with the effort.

'I saw him last week.' He ate the fish, which had been freshly grilled and presented to him by Rosie.

'He did not mention his intention to take another wife to you?' Gertrude sat on a window seat and glanced outside as the carriage disappeared from view.

'No, obviously not.' He drank another mouthful of wine. 'The news is most surprising, madam, because of his lack of comment.'

'Do you ask yourself why?' Her attention had turned back to him.

'No, not really. He was more interested in what is happening in the Inn and the courts in London. So, here I am, asking you.' His voice was calm, but inside his anger grew. She played games with him — why?

'Well, if your father does not want you to be privy to his personal arrangements I am hardly going to break his confidence. Perhaps he avoids your disapproval before it becomes public knowledge. You have a cutting tongue, sir, and are most forthright in expressing it without giving thought to the feelings of your victims. You will do well in court, no doubt.' She stood up. 'Suffice to say he is old enough to make his own decisions about whom he chooses to spend his remaining years with. Besides, once his son returns from boarding school he will need a new mama to see to him. Do not think only of yourself, Gerald. You pined for your own mama after she left this world. You never gave thought to how difficult a role it was to fill, and me, a young widow with my own two girls to support. I will see you at dinner. Do you have a change of clothes with you?' She stopped before the door and waited for a reply.

'Yes, madam, I always carry a change of clothes. I have learned that one should always be prepared for unexpected events.' He lifted his glass to her as she left the room.

'Damn!' he muttered under his breath. What game did she play with him? Why should such a beautiful creature be coerced into a marriage with his father. The thought made him angry; he clenched his fist, balling the napkin and throwing it down on his empty plate as he stood up. If he had not strayed back to this damnable hall, he should have been halfway to Whitby by now to meet the packet which would return him by the Thames to London. Instead, he had rescued the damsel, stumbled across a family secret, and fallen in what? Not love, but he had been captivated by those innocent eyes. Like a bee to a beautiful fragrant flower, he was attracted to this girl and her plight. He smiled. Funny how fate sometimes changes plans and destiny when we least expect it. Looking at the door, he thought of Gertrude. Whatever she was using this girl for, he was about to find out and interfere. He had apologised for his previous outburst because he had indeed been sorry. His father had cut his allowance by half for three months as punishment for it. That was the past. Here and now he needed to keep his wits about him and meddle.

Firstly, he had to find Rosie. She was an amazingly resourceful woman, and he needed to use her resources. His business was about to be unexpectedly and unavoidably delayed.

5

Ellie was anxious to return to her room
— her 'little haven' in the attic; sparse
as it was, it was away from the world.
There, she would try to sort out what
there was to be done about her future.
She realised she must try to talk to the
younger Mr Cookson and explain
herself before the man left the hall with
such an awful opinion of her, returning,
she presumed, to his father to discover
what was being planned.

'Ellie, dear, I wish to speak to you.'
Gertrude was standing in the hallway
after having left the morning room. She
had obviously been waiting for Ellie's
return. The older woman waved her
over, gesturing they should go into the
study together.

Ellie knew straight away that this
would not be an idle chat. It was the
room she had been rebuked and

punished in as a child, and often reproached as a young woman. Gertrude would sit in her husband's old chair behind his desk and try to intimidate her, as she did the servants if they had caused her displeasure.

Cybil and Esme removed their bonnets, spencers and mufflers and went as if to follow Ellie into the study behind Gertrude. They exchanged knowing looks as they stepped forward in unison.

'Girls, you will find refreshments in the morning room. Please wait for me us in there. This will only take a few moments.' She smiled at them, but it was her voice that told them not to press her on her decision. The young women did not look pleased, but nodded dutifully, obeying their mother's wishes.

However, Esme could not resist an attempt at joining in. 'We have so much to tell you, mother. Miss Parkes . . . ' Esme began.

'Later, dear, you must only wait a few

short minutes then you can tell me all your news,' Getrude said.

'Very well. Come Cybil,' Esme replied, before turning and leaving her mother and Ellie alone.

Ellie entered the room she hated between old mahogany doors. They were as hard and as unyielding as her aunt herself could be, she had often thought. Ellie placed her bonnet on the chair just inside the room along with her gloves.

Her aunt seated herself down in the chair opposite, with her back straight and her head held high, she expressed her displeasure. 'Ellie, you have made a very embarrassing presumption. I was quite at a loss as to what to say, or do, to make amends to young Mr Gerald. In view of this, I would ask you to control your impetuous nature. Now, poor young Mr. Gerald has heard the news of your wedding betrothal from you. This is most improper. If his father wishes to remarry, he has the right to choose his own time to tell his own son of his intentions. Can you imagine how foolish you made him, a man grown, feel?' Gertrude looked around the room, as if lost in the humiliation of it all.

Ellie had been preparing herself for a rebuke of her naivety, or stupidity, but she had not thought of this point. Gertrude's words resounded in Ellie's mind. Ellie had not given a thought for what effect — or shock this situation must have had on his son. He must be appalled at the notion that she was to be his new step mother. A young and foolish wench, who he first met as she nearly fell into the river. 'I didn't think about that — sorry! The news is so fresh to me that I have not had time . . . I must go and apologise and make amends . . . '

'See, once again I have to think for you. You are to be a bride — you have to learn to think for yourself — but not just yet. You have proved yourself unready. Whilst Mr Gerald, the younger, is in my home, you will sleep in the smaller guest room, next to my own. You will not talk to the man, unless I am near you or present as a companion. I have already apologised on your behalf and, fortunately, he understands that your eagerness was down to your excitement at the prospect of becoming a wife and nothing more. You will avoid situations where you are alone with him, where you can cause him more grievances. Do you understand me?' She peered at her from across the desk.

'I understand very clearly, Aunt Gertrude,' Ellie said quietly, but in her heart she knew that she would find a way to speak to this man again. Somehow he had to understand she wanted no part in this marriage. But, she wondered, would he really understand? 'Aunt Gertrude, I would like to speak to you about the marriage.'

Her aunt, who was about to stand, sat back down and looked at her, her lips set in a fine line, 'Do you? There will be time for us to sort out the finer details in the coming weeks as I prepare for Christmas in the hall. My life will be full of planning for the next year by the look of it. I have plans in mind and in place for your wedding. You need not fret over it, just leave the details to your poor old aunt and enjoy your time to shine, my girl.' She stood up again, obviously deciding she had dealt with the issue satisfactorily.

'I mean, I wish to discuss the wisdom of it,' Ellie spoke clearly and braced herself for her aunt's response.

'The wisdom of it?' Gertrude repeated. 'Pray tell me what you know of 'wisdom' for if you have such knowledge, you clearly keep it well hidden.' A cloud had descended over the woman as her stare intensified and darkened.

'Exactly my feelings, aunt.' Ellie knew what she was about to declare would throw Gertrude into a foul mood, so she framed her words carefully. 'I am younger than this gentleman, so much so that his own son is older than me by at least five summers.'

'Years, Ellie, eight years, what of it?' Gertrude snapped.

'I am not worldly, aunt. I can not think how I could make such a man happy . . .'

Getrude laughed. 'Well, we agree on one point at least, you can not think!'

Ellie ignored the insult and continued in her conciliatory tone. 'I fear I would only annoy the man. Therefore, I wish to politely decline this marriage proposal, discreetly of course, before it is made public. I do not want to cause further embarrassment to anyone. Then he would be able to find a more suitable companion, equal to the task.' Ellie watched as her aunt slowly stood straight, rested a hand on the desk as she composed herself and then walked around the desk until she was standing in front of Ellie.

'I could accuse you of being an ungrateful child. I could say that for all your years of living off my compassion, sharing my home as another daughter, after I took you in despite being the unwanted brat, deserted by a wanton woman — Oh, yes, do not worry on that point, for your fiancé knows the detail of your mother's shame. Yet, he has agreed to take you into his home, to be as mother to his children, to tend his own dear mother in her failing years and to share his name, his wealth and his future. Yet, you in your 'wisdom',' her voice gradually started to rise until she was almost shouting into Ellie's face, 'you, in your new found wisdom think you have the choice to turn away a man of his standing!' She let out a long breath. 'You would be insulting both me as your guardian and him as your future to think so. Since when has anything in marriage been equal? It is time you grew up, Ellie, and faced a few facts.' She breathed deeply before continuing in a calmer note. 'Or, I could put these selfish sentiments down to the pre-wedding nerves young women often have and that in fact you are just a little daunted at your sudden change of circumstances.' The thin lips turned up slightly at the corners, as if making an attempt to smile. 'The latter is of course understandable, desirable and will pass — quickly. The former, if it were a true reflection of your thinking, could only result in the withdrawal of my patronage.' She leaned forward slightly. 'You own nothing. You have no income. You have nowhere else to go, so that viewpoint would end in folly and a life of wanton poverty, no doubt as your mother will have ended her days. Now, Ellie, which viewpoint is correct? Are you an ungrateful wretch or a nervous maid?'

Ellie did not flinch. She smiled as sweetly as she could. 'The news is fresh, Aunt. Perhaps I could meet the man, so we could better understand each other, and then I can settle my maiden's nerves.'

Gertrude patted her shoulder as she turned her towards the door, the meeting was over. 'Good girl, perhaps you have a modicum of wisdom in that head of yours after all. Let me give you one piece of advice which will help you in life. Whilst you have your youth and your looks and a firm healthy body, use the assets you have been blessed with to secure a financially secure future. Looks do not last long when one has to live in poverty.' She opened the doors. 'We shall join my girls and then I think I would like you to read to me.'

Ellie followed her aunt across the hall. She was stifling the urge to run through the main entrance and keep running. To feel the air on her face and shake off the invisible shackles which kept her tied to a hall and a life she increasingly hated. But the old witch was right; she had no means to live on beyond the charity of the woman whose back her eyes currently bore holes in. She needed time to think, to plan, to decide how she should escape without ending up as her own poor mother apparently had. Ellie wondered if the same desire to be free had driven the woman to an act of sheer destruction, and if, as they surmised, she fell to the lowest existence a woman can. Ellie wanted to believe that, despite the war, her mother had found her happiness and freedom — but most of all love. The only part of the story which hurt her was that she, as an infant, had not shared her journey. Then she remembered Gertrude's comments about poverty and persuaded herself that she had been saved from starving to death by her mother's act of sacrifice by leaving her with her husband's family.

★ ★ ★

Dinner that evening was taken with her aunt in her own room. Mr Cookson shared the meal down stairs with Cybil and Esme. Gertrude had sent down her excuses that she was not feeling quite herself, but did not feel like being alone, so they would have to excuse Ellie, also.

The next day Ellie was asked to read to her aunt, walk with her aunt, eat with her aunt, play cards with her . . . until no further chance existed for her to walk outside the building or even go to the servants' quarters to speak to Cook and therefore escape to hopefully, catch Mr Cookson in the stables before he went out for his ride. It was impossible to be in his presence at all, whilst Esme and Cybil talked, walked and ate with him whenever he ventured back to the hall. Three days went by and it was clear from the odd remark made to her aunt, that Mr Cookson was becoming restless and would soon leave. Ellie realised that, if he did, her aunt had somehow won.

Ellie was even told to retire at the same time as her aunt. At the end of what Ellie felt was the longest day of her life, she saw to it that her aunt was comfortable in bed, having read to her again. Then, as ordered no doubt, Rosie made sure that Ellie was in hers. Only this evening she had come to Ellie first, before entering Gertrude's room. The maid was carrying a small tray with a bottle of medicine upon it, along with a silver spoon, towards the door to Gertrude's bedchamber.

'What is that, Rosie?' Ellie asked.

'This,' she held up the tray, 'Oh, this is madam's sleeping medicine. If she doesn't take this now, she don't sleep good, and you know what she is like when she is vexed. This keeps her sweeter,' she whispered, and then chuckled.

'Does it take long to work?' Ellie asked.

'No, miss, why? Does you want some?' Rosie offered her the bottle.

'No, I just wondered. Goodnight, Rosie,' she said.

'Good night, miss.' She hesitated. 'I'm sorry, miss, that the marriage wasn't to young Mr Gerald. I know I am speaking out of turn, but he is a good sort. You'd do well with him.'

'You know him, Rosie?' Ellie had not realised that she could find out more about her stranger from Rosie, but of course she could. Perhaps, Ellie wondered, she might be able to take a message to him for her.

'Oh, I know him well enough. I saw him grow from a babe to a young man. He used to live here after his mama died. Lovely she was. She left him her mother's money which is how he funded his move to London and them law courts. He's done well, miss . . . despite his troubled childhood.'

'Rosie!' Gertrude's voice resounded around the room from her bedchamber.

'Sorry, miss.' She winked at Ellie then shouted back, 'Coming ma'am!' Rosie walked toward the other room.

'Rosie, could you . . . ?'

'Not now, lass, I want to live to see morning.' She left.

Ellie waited till she had heard Rosie leave her aunt's room. Then she waited longer until she heard the first of many snores. She took her shawl from the chair, wrapped it around her shoulders and climbed the steps to her window. Silently, she opened it wide and stepped out in slipper covered feet, walking out onto her ledge, which would take her to her own special place.

There, leaning against the roof she stared at her favourite star, and then closed her eyes. The night air, fresh on her face, heightened her senses. She felt momentarily free from all restrictions. 'I asked to be loved, and you played me for a fool, why?' she whispered to herself.

'I didn't know that I had, miss,' a deep voice answered her. Ellie, startled, stood straight up, nearly losing her balance. A strong arm circled her waist, pulling her back to safety, holding her firmly. She found herself pinned to the roof by Mr Gerald Cookson.

Her breath deepened with the shock of his sudden appearance. His presence unexpected, surprised her; her near fall had scared her, and his body resting against hers, as he made her steady and safe again, caused another surge of emotions to stir within her soul, befuddling her senses even more.

She swallowed, unable to speak for a moment as he leaned over her delicate frame, shielding her from the danger of the fall.

'Are you all right, Ellie? I should not have been so foolish as to speak out like that, but I was surprised that you had managed to follow me here. Or that you were so daring as to try. This is a very high and dangerous place, Ellie.'

His face was so near hers, that she could feel the warmth of his breath on the flesh of her cheek. His hand rested on her waist as her shawl had cascaded to her feet as she reacted to his voice. Through the fine cotton of her nightgown she could feel his grip: firm, warm and secure.

'I did not follow you, sir. I had no way of knowing you would be out here at this hour. How could I have?' She was still whispering, despite the fact that they were on a roof with the whole night to themselves.

'You discovered my secret place then. I thought I had seen an angel on the roof, the other night when I walked the path of my childhood in the woods, but then I saw you in the flesh and realised that, in a way, I was right, but this angel has substance.'

'Your place? I come here to be alone.' She was staring into his deep brown eyes. 'How is it yours?' she asked quietly.

'I used to sit out here as a child; it was easy to reach from my room in the attic. Sometimes I wanted to run away or stay on the roof. Hide from them, make believe that they had been taken away and when I returned my mother and father would be there waiting for me: my previous life restored. I suppose that sounds like the rantings of a madman.' His face was so near to hers she could feel his warmth, and smell his musk.

'The attic room is usually my room,' she whispered. 'I was moved out of it in order to accommodate your preference it seems.'

'No, Ellie, Gertrude would deliberately put me there to keep me in my place. I have annoyed her by staying here.'

'Why have you?' Ellie asked, aware of feeling uneasy sensations as he made no effort to move his body away from hers, yet kept talking to her as if they were seated in the morning room and all was correct and proper.

'Curiosity,' he replied, and smiled down at her.

'Curiosity about what?' she asked.

'You,' his reply was simple and to the point.

Ellie suddenly became self conscious. 'Sir, please move your hand?' she asked.

He did, and slid it slowly along her side. His eyes stared down into hers. Ellie opened her mouth to speak to him, to tell him she meant him to remove his hand from her body, when she found she could not get the words out. His lips covered hers, as he kissed her tenderly, at the same time she felt the gentle motion of his hand moving further and further up her body, over her ribs until he found the contour of her breast, where his fingers cupped and fondled their prize. Ellie's mind told her to push him away, but if she did, he would fall. Her body was definitely telling her something else. She closed her eyes as the kiss became more urgent; the sensations as he stroked her flesh through the thin fabric of her nightdress intensified the pleasure of this intimate and spontaneous embrace, followed by the well of emotions that rose within her own body. Ellie slipped her arms inside his jacket. She could feel his muscle through his shirt as she returned the embrace, holding his torso close to her own — loving the feeling of intimacy it brought and shamelessly longing for more of it. He lifted his head up from hers and looked down into her sapphire eyes. The stroking movement of his hand slowly ceased as they stared at both other, each seeming equally surprised by the ease of their reactions.

'Sir, I meant, could you remove your hand from my body,' she spoke softly and, somewhat reluctantly, removed her arms from around his body.

'Did you? I think your actions would say otherwise.'

She could not look straight back at him. He leaned back against the roof slates next to her, so he too could stare up at the stars.

'You must not think that I . . . Mr Cookson, you caught me by surprise. I was . . . ' She was lost for words, how could she say she did not, had not, experienced such intimacy before, or explain that she had been talking to the stars?

'You had been talking to yourself . . . Speaking prayers aloud perhaps? I am sorry I interrupted such private thoughts. How do you expect to find love by marrying my father, Ellie? No matter what Gertrude may have said to you, you do not know this man. He is no ogre, but he is not right for you. You are young, fit and have warmth in your body and soul . . . ' He flicked a curl which had fallen over her cheek. 'You are desirable. He is . . . no longer as desirable as perhaps he once was, except in his wallet perhaps.' He turned his head to face her.

Ellie looked back at him, a stranger, who shared her special place on the roof and had made her aware of such feelings that should shame her. She reached down for her shawl and wrapped it around her body as; exposed to the night air she felt the chill left after his body had ceased to shield her. 'Is that what you think of me? You think I would . . . would trade my youth, my . . . body for his money? You may think what you like, sir, I am not the woman you think I am. I have no defence, as my actions have been shameful, confirming this image in your mind no doubt, which I can not justify or undo. I can assure you though that I do not want your father or his money. I knew nothing of my aunt's intentions until just before you arrived. I do not want to marry an old man . . . or any man I do not know or love. I want . . . Never mind, it is none of your business. Goodnight!'

She inched away from him to return, but he reached out his hand and prevented her moving further by placing the flat of his hand upon her stomach, before she had a chance to regain her balance and find her way back along the ledge.

'You have no idea what I think of you, Ellie, as we have not been at liberty to discuss the matter. However, you may have an equally jaded view of me. Calm yourself, do not be frightened of me or of your future. Certainly, feel no shame for being young and alive. We have both acted, I think, out of our normal character, for I am no cad. I make no habit of soliciting wenches upon a roof top.' He grinned at her at the absurdity of their situation, she thought, rather than mocking her. 'We have such things in common, you and me, yet there are many aspects of our personalities and lives which are very different facets that I would love to explore. There is something not right about this matter of the marriage and I intend to find out what it is — other than the obvious unsuitability of either party to its union.'

She was breathing deeply, his hand on her made her feel uneasy in what she could only describe as a pleasant and desirable way. This man was dangerous, not because of what he said, but what he could do to her. She lost control of her senses when they were close. How could she look upon him in a maternal sense? The situation was ridiculous beyond her imagination. No wonder he thought her 'unsuitable'. His father was a man of position, he had respect within the community, and she ran around rooftops, talking to a strange man in little more than a nightshift.

'Tomorrow, I shall leave here and pay another visit to my father. I will find out what I can and I shall return to the hall once more as soon as I have learned the truth of it. You can meet me here the night of my return and we shall talk openly to each other then.' He smiled and removed his hand from her body.

'I can not go through with a marriage to a man who I do not know and who is so much more 'mature' than I, but I have no means to walk away from it as my aunt has clearly pointed out to me. I marry or my life will be in ruins.' She looked up at the sky as if trying to discern a path to freedom. 'Perhaps I should just leave here and seek work elsewhere.' She bit her lip, the suggestion bordered on desperation for she had no references to stand for her reputation and no money of her own to travel far enough away from the hall to consider it a safe distance from her aunt's domineering grasp.

'No, Ellie, that you must never do! Stay here and wait for me to return. Promise me this for I can only go with a clear mind if it is not thinking of what horrendous fate has befallen an unworldly girl, with no clear prospects of her own . . . ' His smile had vanished to be replaced by concern.

'A few days more,' she said, uncertain if she could follow through on her suggestion anyway. Unworldly described her accurately, although 'girl' was not a description she liked under the circumstances. She had never felt more like a woman in her life than in the last half an hour of it.

★ ★ ★

'You wait for me, and I shall return to you. But Ellie, take care, watch what is happening in this house and be aware. Your aunt is a driven woman; once she has her heart set on something happening, she will go to any length to see her wishes come to fruition.'

She nodded, for she knew at least these words were true.

'Please don't think that I am . . . I do not know the truth of my mother's circumstances and Aunt Gertrude takes delight in besmirching her name. I am certain there will have been more to her story than the dire image which is portrayed about her. My actions here . . . Your actions . . . I must . . . '

Without finishing her statement she pulled away from him and left him, leaving Gerald staring at her as she drifted back into the hall.

* * *

Gerald leaned back and looked up at the stars, his mouth remembering the feel of the stolen kiss he had taken from her. Remembering the sensation of her lips against his. How could he look upon her as his father's new bride? The old man would make a fool of himself if he took her as a wife and she would be destined to a life of servitude, worse than a life with Gertrude. One thing he knew for sure; his father could never satisfy her in any way. The match was doomed. No, it could not be. He would return and talk some sense into his father, before it was too late. Thomas, his stepbrother might well take to the young and pretty Ellie, but not with his father. It was too much of a contrast. One staid and set in their ways, the other young, eager to discover new sensations and burning to live. He had felt it in her, it would be a light extinguished by the restrictive life her father would offer her under the watchful gaze of his grandmother. The old bat had killed off Amelia's drive for life; he would not let her do it to another. Where Gertrude fitted into this, he did not know. He had thought Ellie to be a gold-digger, but now he realised she was no more than a young woman who was being used as a puppet in her aunt's plans, but why? Gertude cared nothing for the girl, of that he was sure, so she was securing her what on paper would be a good match. He did not know the truth, but he would find out. He closed his eyes for a moment and visualised Ellie dancing in the grand assemblies in London, with those exquisite golden curls and her delicate features; moving in a classical Greek dress, fine fabric showing those exquisite contours off to perfection. A gust of wind blew bringing him out of his musings — reluctantly, because it was an image he would like to see in reality. If not the father's wife, she would make a beautiful mistress for the son, if she did take after her mother. That is, of course, if the mother's reputation had not been enhanced or besmirched by Gertrude's skill at weaving words.

6

Gerald breakfasted early the next morning. He wanted to speak with his father and face the man who had kept such an important piece of information from him. Their relationship may have been fraught at times; however, he would like to think that his own father could be bothered to tell him when he hoped to remarry. Sometimes it was as if he did not want to see his own and eldest son. This had hurt Gerald junior for years until he realised the sad reason for this. His son was the male image of his first love — his first wife.

Time had passed by since then, the man had remarried but never given the lovely timid Amelia the tenderness she needed and deserved. His father had become cold and divisive, benefitting from the marriage into a respectable older family of the county, yet giving nothing of himself to the woman, other than managing to beget Thomas. The second child, after nine cold years of union, took her mother with her to her grave, leaving her father alone once more except, of course, for the companionship of a devoted elderly mother. Perhaps, Gerald thought, if he told him that he had been staying with Gertrude, he would automatically offer the news with a rational explanation of why it seemed to have slipped his mind on his previous visit. Then he would begin to understand his apparent madness.

Rosie brought in the grilled trout rolled in oats, and placed the plate on the table before him.

'I know it is your favourite dish, sir, and it was caught fresh this morning, just as you like them to be.' She winked at him. 'See my eyes may be not as good as they were, but my memory is just as sharp as it can be. Remember when the squire caught you poaching on his land? I thought you would not sit down again for a week after ma'am had finished caning you.' She looked pitifully at him.

'Yes, I remember it well.' There was no humour in his words.

'Best to let bygones be bygones, no use dwelling on things in the past. She is older now and will very soon be a lonely woman as her daughters both move out. I'm sorry, sir, I should have known better than to mention it to you, sorry.'

'No matter, it's a fine fish.'

He did not ask who caught it or where from. But fresh trout was still a favourite dish of his. Poaching was as rife in the area as smuggling, everyone knew about it and did their part, but nobody told the authorities of how widespread it was.

'Rosie, stay here a while and talk to me, please.' He saw her glance at the door, hesitating as to whether she should stay or go.

'Well, if you order me to, sir, how can

I say no?' She came back to the end of the table.

'Tell me as much as you know about Ellie, and this marriage proposal to my father.'

'She is madam's niece, by her brother Bertram. Her mother was said to be a rare beauty, with fine yellow curls just like Ellie has. I never saw her myself. They were in France when Mr Bertie met her. The child was sent home because of the troubles that broke out, the woman chose to stay with her lover, apparently. Bertram died fighting his enemy. That is all we were ever told by the family, sir. Ellie was no more than four when she arrived here, so young, so fragile. You had not been gone more than two seasons. So she remembers none of what happened and never met you before, although she, in a way, took your place and attic room. She has no memories of her poor parents for that matter. She has seen portraits of Captain Bertram, but none of her mama, because Gertrude destroyed the miniature he kept of his 'foolish' wife. It was sent to Gertude amongst other personal belongings which she kept in her room in what had been her brother's military chest. It was intact until this last season anyway. As for the marriage, it has only just been announced. That is all I know, sir. She is a pretty, young lass, quick and would make any young man a fine wife, sir . . . Don't you think so, sir?' She tilted her head on one side and stared at him.

'Now, Rosie, I think you are meddling.' He reprimanded her lightly and grinned at her.

'Me, sir? Never, sir!'

'Where is it now, this chest?' he asked, as he finished his meal and stood up.

'Well, the chest remains in the room, madam's room, that is, but some of the papers from it were removed recently. I don't really know for sure, but I think you might find they was sent to your father earlier in the year. Jason, the stable lad saw them, he was dusting out the carriage for madam. Mrs Hemmings had put them on the seat then remembered something to say to Samuel, before she got in it. The lad, being slow at his task had knocked them onto the carriage floor and they slipped out of their wallet. He quickly put them back in and replaced them where Madam had left them. Then Gertrude saw him near the carriage as he was backing away. Well! You never heard such a reprimand as that lad got. We know she has a temper on her, but you would have thought he'd tried to steal the crown jewels, bless him. What she would have done if she'd seen him touch her things, well I dread to think,' she whispered. 'Just as well that cane of hers was not handy.'

'What were the documents? Could he tell what they were?'

'No, sir, he couldn't read, but he said the words looked different somehow, and the paper was stiff and painted around the edges. Even the ribbon looked grand. It could have been

Bertam's commissions or whatever they have. She grabbed up the wallet and sat holding it. Samuel said she still had tight a grip on them when he arrived in Gorebeck. The lad said that Samuel, the ostler, told him they had gone to Gorebeck to her cousin's place. Not his house, as she usually did to see Amelia, and deal with her affairs in the comfort of their home with your father, but instead she went direct to his offices in town. Of course, he had to wait outside, but them papers was left there.' Rosie glanced at the door as if she expected Gertrude to burst in at any moment. 'This must have been at the beginning of the year, sir. Because it had not been long since Mrs Amelia had died giving birth to the wee bairn . . . Sad day that was when the news arrived. She didn't visit too frequently, but always smiled freely when anyone saw her.'

'Why would this have been commented upon? My father would surely be interested in the family paperwork.' He looked at her; her cheeks had flushed slightly, a simple sign that told him she knew there was something not right here also.

'Well, I got to thinking on it. Why did she never tell the lass that she had anything of her parents' things in her possession? She has been kept here with little of her own. She does her aunt's bidding and is brought out for show when folk visit, so long as she don't overshadow her cousins. You know how Gertrude made you feel, indebted like, when you were a young lad, well that is what she does to that girl. Now she is expected to marry without question — or rhyme or reason. I tell you it ain't right nor fair to the lass. She shouldn't be packaged off to your father, she should be matched proper to someone of her own age, or at least near to it, perhaps a little older and more worldly wise — it ain't right! But who is going to help her out of it? Tell me that young sir — who?' Rosie stopped abruptly; her tone had changed although her volume had not. She had been carried away and lost all sense of boundary, forgetting who she was talking to — the man, no longer a boy. Her colour deepened. 'I forget myself. I apologise. I meant no offence to your father, sir. It is just after seeing how Mrs Amelia paled . . . I wonder what will become of Ellie. She has spirit, but it has never been allowed to fly free,' she muttered as she gathered up his plate.

'You care for her. Tell me, and do not take offence at the question, she has a wildness to that spirit you also have recognised. Do you think she has inherited her mother's tendencies? Do you think she would enjoy the life of a well kept mistress in London?' He saw the instant change in Rosie's face. Her lips tightened into a firm line.

Rosie's head shot around. 'If I wasn't just a common maid . . . If you was not a gentleman . . . How could you say such a thing? She is better than that and apparently better than the person who would think it! Excuse me, sir, I have an honest days work to do as honest decent folk do!' She stormed toward the door.

'Rosie . . . wait a minute . . . I was only asking your opinion . . . '

'You got it . . . sir!' replied Rosie, as she disappeared out of the room.

Rosie did not stop, she left in a fluster. Gerald felt awkwardly embarrassed, he grinned, though, at his own folly and presumption. He had been given his answer, but he would have to make amends with the woman because he had fond memories of her and would not have offended her for the world, despite her being just a servant. She had been the one human being to offer genuine comfort to him when he had been a frightened lonely child.

He left the room, passing Esme in the hallway who greeted him coolly.

'Is your mother up yet, Esme?' he asked, as he collected his Garrick from the hook by the door.

She tilted her head high and smiled at him. 'No, she rests, some days she feels very tired and needs more sleep

118

— nothing to worry about, she has much to contemplate and arrange for our futures. Can I give her a message?' She smiled, but he realised she was merely being her curious, or rather nosy, self.

'Yes, tell her that I thank her for her hospitality, but must leave here today.' He nodded politely as if to take his leave of her after swinging his coat onto his shoulders.

'Of course, Gerald. Will we see you again before the wedding?' Esme asked, as he walked to the door.

'I can not say.' His answer was honest, as he had no wish to see her or the wedding. If he could find a way he would not let the wedding go ahead. Somehow it would be stopped, without his father or the girl being embarrassed or hurt. He had to move quickly, though, before it was announced and the knowledge was placed in the public domain.

He nodded politely at her then headed for the stables. He had business to discuss with his father, the sooner the better. Rosie's outbursts had given him much to think about, beyond the golden curls, an exquisite face and, as he glanced at his hands he was filled with memories of the sensuous feel of the warmth of her welcoming flesh through the soft fabric of her night-dress. It was a delicious memory that he could not shake off. These were darkened at the thought of such loveliness being presented to his father as his property.

Jason was working hard, as usual, brushing out the area where the coach usually stood.

'Mornin', sir,' the lad said, as he diligently continued with his work.

'Good morning, Jason. Where has the carriage gone?' he asked, out of curiosity, as he walked over to the stall where his horse was kept.

'Madam ordered it right early she did. Samuel moaned like mad . . . not within her earshot of course. Sorry, sir, I mean his belly was none too good last night . . . that was what he moaned about, not madam.' The lad looked anxiously at him.

'Do you know where she was going?' Gerald swung the saddle onto the horse's back.

'Not sure, sir, although I did hear her say something about Gorebeck to Samuel, but when I asked him he said it was none of my business.' There was an impish look in his eyes. 'He don't always talk friendly when his gut rumbles.'

'And so, it isn't.' Gerald walked his horse out onto the cobblestoned yard tossing the lad a coin for his inquisitive nature. 'When I return, and I will do, Jason, you tell me what else you hear that is not your business. If it is interesting I will reward you well.'

The lad smiled.

'Tell me, do you remember the day you knocked some of madam's papers off the coach's seat . . . '

The lad's eyes widened. 'She saw me?' he replied.

'No, lad, you would have known if she had before now. I should think you have felt her cane before now.'

The lad nodded and Gerald felt for him, as he had known the sting of a beating in his own youth. 'Tell me what you saw, Jason.'

'Papers, with a ribbon, fine ribbon and a seal with a small bird on it. Fancy they was, gold and green pattern on the edge. Can't read, sir, but they looked right grand. I had to get them back right quick, afore madam saw.'

'Keep those eyes and ears open and we shall speak again.'

'Yes, sir,' the lad said. He pocketed his coin and watched Gerald ride apace for Gorebeck.

* * *

Ellie rose early after a very fitful sleep. With all her heart she had tried to feel ashamed of her physical feelings as she remembered those few stolen moments of intimacy with the handsome,

122

younger Mr Cookson. Her behaviour was shameful, yet she had felt alive in every pore of her being in a way that she had never experienced before. It was, as she had discovered, what she longed for — to be free of the hall and experience life as a woman with such a man. What concerned her was not her sensations, but what Mr Gerald Cookson, the younger, really thought of her.

Could she trust him? Dare she trust him? Was she about to make the same mistake her own mother had by falling in love at the touch of a man's hand? The idea was simply ludicrous as her mother had had a husband already — her father. He had been her father, but what he or her mother were really like she had no way of knowing. Both had left her. Her mother had been an experienced woman, not an impressionable young maid.

Ellie shook her head to try to clear her mind. She wanted no thoughts of pity, least of all from herself. That led to low spirits. She would find her own way. Ellie decided that she would talk to him again, when he returned — if he returned to the hall. If he thought badly of her then she would have to face up to her own shame and her aunt's wrath, again. Cookson seemed an enigma to her; she could not determine what he was really like as their acquaintance was so short. Had he played with her emotions to spite his own father? She had heard of such things happening between father and son. Or had he been testing her to see if she were fit to be in his father's house, let alone take the position of his wife. He may see her as a threat upon his inheritance, if she was seeking his father's fortune to spend. Did the son want to protect the elder? The whole situation was intolerable. She did not want to be a respectable wife to an older man. Ellie knew she could no more give herself to the father than she could bear to live in the hall any longer with her insufferable cousins and her overbearing aunt. Ellie could not spend her days thinking of how intimate she had been with the son and he with her, than she could bear the thought of never knowing the son further. She dressed, deciding it was better to be busy than dwelling on too many unknown answers to impossible questions, and then she went downstairs to breakfast with her aunt.

'There you are, Ellie,' Esme greeted her as she stepped off the last stair into the entrance hall.

'Is your mama still abed?' Ellie asked, as she entered the morning room, hopeful that she may well be. A table was laid ready for their breakfast. She seated herself at it, noting there were only two places set.

'No, she has gone out early this morning, Ellie. She has much to see to and no time to waste.' Esme joined her, and then helped herself to a portion of coddled eggs. 'These are hardly warm. I must speak with Rosie. Yesterday they were not seasoned. I swear that woman is getting too old to do her work.'

'Has Cybil accompanied her?' Ellie asked, changing the subject. She knew too well Rosie was not as efficient as she once was, but she had always been there. Ellie worried about what would become of the woman. Snapping her mind back to the immediate problems in her own life she wondered what business had roused her aunt so early in the day. It must have been important to get her out of bed so early.

'Yes, Mama would hardly travel alone. So there we are, just the two of us to entertain ourselves for the whole day. Won't that be entertaining?' she smiled at Ellie, sweetly.

'Indeed, but don't forget, there is also Mr Cookson to entertain,' Ellie added, with a sudden surge of emotions as she cheered at the prospect of seeing him again, despite Esme's presence.

'I am afraid not. He has already left. He rose and breakfasted really early, and left without as much as a by your leave. I wonder if Rosie managed to keep his food warm. I cannot begin to see how that man fares in the Courts and Inns of London. He is quite coarse. He has forgotten everything that Mama taught him before he went to boarding school. One would have hoped they could have turned him into a gentleman.' She leaned over to Ellie. 'His father is said to despair of his 'habits'.'

'Really,' Ellie responded, not wanting to encourage her to expand her limited knowledge of the man further, for she knew what a gossip Esme was and Ellie wanted to find out the truth herself.

'Yes, absolutely. It is said that he and Miss Parkes have had a 'liaison' and that is why he had to be sent away from the area. Can you imagine the scandal, if their liaison had become public! Ask yourself this, Ellie, why else does he not work with his father? Both are men of the law, and why has Miss Parkes, a pleasant enough looking woman with a small fortune to her name, not secured herself a fine young man for a husband? That is just one of his dalliances. I am sure that whilst in London he has turned the head and flipped the skirt up of many a fine maid, no doubt bragging about it in his club afterwards. I've been shown his type before when we were in London. You can easily see what they are like by the way they look at their next innocent victim. They toy with a maid's emotions and anything else the maid will allow them to. It really is . . . '

Ellie stood up. 'You must excuse me, Esme. I feel that I need some fresh air to clear my head this morning.' She walked out of the room, hearing Esme's voice.

'Of course, dear,' spoken softly behind her, but not seeing the look of satisfaction upon her cousin's face.

7

Ellie had to make the break from her cousin's presence and feel the open air around her. She could not sit there listening to such words wondering if Esme was trying to scare her off him, or if she had now developed the ability to read her mind. She was certain that the woman knew nothing of her intimate moment with Gerald, but the doubts had come crashing into her mind. Had she been 'toyed' with as a fool? If Esme's opinion and knowledge of men was correct then was it obvious to all but her that he had set his sights upon her. All she wanted was love and the right to be her own person. She would wait a few days and see if he returned to the hall as he said he would. If he did not, then she would pack her few belongings and leave.

Gertrude and Cybil arrived at the outskirts of Gorebeck at her cousin's home.

'Cybil, you must go and see how my aunt fairs. She is devoted to her dear Gerald. Whilst I see to my business dear, keep her entertained for me,' she said quietly and daughter nodded at her mother knowing only too well that she needed her distracting whilst Gertrude spoke to Gerald in private.

Gertrude proceeded toward the dining room where her cousin had broken his morning fast. He left his dining room and greeted her by the doorway to his study.

'Gertie, my dear.' He placed an arm around her waist and showed her inside his personal room. Half of the room was given over to a large mahogany desk, shelves filled with legal books, racks of files and two sturdy leather winged chairs. In the other half of the room a fire glowed warm, two softer cushioned chairs were placed either side of the hearth, and he escorted Gertrude to one of these. 'You have travelled to see me early in the day, Gertie.' He closed the door behind them once she was comfortably seated and then opened a corner cabinet with a little key which he kept on his chain, attached to his waistcoat.

'Gregory, we may have a problem.' She placed a hand on the arm of the chair and turned to face him.

'In what way, my love?' he asked, as he removed a decanter of sherry from the cupboard and poured two quite large glasses out for them.

'Honestly, Gerald, that child of yours! He has been to the hall and seen Eléanor. I fear he will cause problems and deliberately disrupt our plans; you know how impossible he can be, Gerald. What is worse is that she, on meeting him, thought him to be you. She made it quite clear that she presumed him to be her suitor and was obviously open to the notion. If only his arrival had not coincided with the very day that I chose to tell her of the match.' She shook her head. 'Fate can play tricks on us when we least expect it, Gerald.'

Gerald placed the crystal glass in her hand and she sipped it as if savouring nectar.

'I do not see that there is a problem, Gertrude. Why would she care if it is he or I who she is to marry. She has surely been told of my position. He is not offering his hand for her, I am. She has few, if any choices to make any match save to a peddler or game keeper! He will no doubt be put out that I did not think to divulge my plans to him when he was here last. I shall merely tell him that I was uncertain whether I should go ahead and needed to see her for a few days to be sure. He has plenty to occupy his mind in London, he will not ponder on it long. Mark my words, Gertrude, he will soon tire of life here. If Eléanor is as beautiful as you say she is, then he is merely put out that his old father has netted himself a catch, when his own success has not found him a match he is comfortable with.' He sat in the chair opposite her and drank his sherry. 'This should be savoured when wanted and not when people decide is the hour to drink it, don't you agree, Gertie?'

'I always agree with you, my dear, but I want you to change your plans. Young Gerald, has an inquisitive mind, he likes to stir me. He has not forgiven me for trying so hard to take his dear mama's place in his life.' She looked at the fire and sniffed.

'Now, Gertie, he was a selfish boy and has long since grown into a fine young man. His selfish streak will take him to the city where your young ward will be no great beauty. He can afford to buy the favours of the women he wants. She is merely a diversion who has upset his pride because he had not had previous knowledge. He told me he was returning via the packet at Whitby. If I had realised he was going to stop by the hall I would have sent him to Harrogate on business instead and asked him to take the stagecoach from there.'

'I want you to forget the banns, forget the grand announcement of an engagement at Christmas. I want you to arrange a special licence. You are on excellent terms with Bishop Windam, explain you wish the marriage to go ahead so that you can show your new bride off at the Christmas Ball, at the hall, invite him to attend. He likes a good feast. Then their will be no time for Young Gerald to upset things and all we be set in place. Once married, we only need to wait for the legalities to come through, then all will be as it should have been these long years. In the mean time you have all the benefits a new bride can bring to your home, your mother will have a companion and nurse, Thomas a mother when he returns from St Andrews on holiday, my girls will have left the hall and our futures will be secure.'

He looked at her for a moment, thoughtfully. 'Gertrude, do you think she will she agree without question?' he asked, after draining the bottom of his glass.

'Yes, she will. I have put years of my life into raising that child and securing our future. By the time I have prepared her, she will definitely agree. However, I need you to send Young Gerald away. She needs no distractions.'

'Then, you acted in haste, my dear. That is not like you. Surely, you are not having 'doubts', Gertie. That would be folly.' He leaned forward and held out his hand to her. She took it in hers and squeezed his soft fingers tenderly.

'I have waited so long for this, Gerald and now we are so near. That boy has always interfered. He caused his own mother to perish and has never shown gratitude to me for taking him in when you were starting out with your career. If only your father had not forced you to marry her, our lives would have been very different.' She stared at him, his round face with ruddy thread-veined cheeks, were now coloured with the warmth from the fire, the taste of sherry and the flush of emotions, he rarely showed anyone else. She stared at what had once been a fine handsome jaw line. My love, these women have not been strong enough for you. They have left you all alone . . . ' She swallowed, her normally hard complexion softened by the warmth of a fire, the mellow drink that revived her aching body from the jolting of the coach and the sight of the face she so adored.

'Now, Gertie, there is no use going over the past. We are both here now. This marriage will change everything. You know it. So stop worrying. I will deal with my son. He has commitments in London. If the lass has any doubts about the match, then have that old maid of yours prepare a drink with some of your medicine in it. Enough so she is amiable but not asleep.' He smiled. 'She only needs to calm herself, until we are married. Once she is my wife, she has all the time in the world to accustom herself to her new position. But I will not have a maid dictate to me my life or my future. Now, I will insist you take a rest here before you return home. I will send Samuel to town on an errand to purchase some supplies for you, your Cybil will be busy with Mama for some time so freshen yourself up and then I will come up and see you shortly.' He smiled at her and she leaned forward and kissed his forehead gently. 'I will join you very shortly, my love, now go and make yourself comfortable.'

He opened the door. 'Lizzie, take my Mrs Hemmings to the willow guest room, she needs to take a rest. See to it that she is not disturbed.'

Gertrude, stern faced as ever came out of the study. She hardly looked at Gerald as she walked past him to the stairs where the upper house maid waited to escort her to the bedchamber.

'This way, ma'am,' she said and gestured for Gertrude to follow her.

'Samuel!' Gerald shouted.

'Yes, sir,' the man entered the hall way from outside the front door.

'Take the coach to Gorebeck. I want you to go to the butchers and pick up a side of lamb for the hall. Make sure he also gives you my usual order. Tell Mr Gumble to put it on my account.' He passed him a few coins, 'Take a drink at the inn whilst you are there and return in three hours or so.'

'Yes, sir,' Samuel said looking very pleased.

Gerald stared up the stairs and smiled. Life was coming good again, he thought as he returned to his study, his business yet to finish.

8

Ellie walked briskly along the road which by-passed the estate. She had dressed in her walking boots, coat and hat, with no idea in her head as to where she was going except as far away from Esme's taunts as she could. She veered off the road and followed a track which cut through the forest, heading away from their own lands.

She seemed to trip, stumble and nearly fall as she finally reached the far side of the forest to view the open fields and moorland beyond them. Ellie realised that she must have walked over five miles and was starting to feel thirsty, hungry and tired. Wishing she had managed to eat more of her meal before leaving the hall, she stopped to catch her breath, regain her composure and think clearly before going any further. She had left with no coin, possessions or victuals; the only thing of substance she had swallowed was her pride — but for the last time. On her own and with no clear destination in mind Ellie had boldly stepped out into the world, totally unprepared. She had, as her aunt would say, acted very foolishly. Foolishly or not, she could not help but admire the view over gentle moorland as she stared towards the edge of the vale. The fields fell away in the distance to the gentler land below where villages nestled. It was as she followed her eye line that she saw a familiar house peeking out from above the treetops at the head of the vale. The chimney stacks of Penny Manor, the home of Miss Parkes, peered out of the greenery as if inviting her to come closer and make an unannounced visit. I wonder, she thought to herself as she contemplated a long dismal journey back to the old hall, or dare herself to continue on her reckless path to this intriguing woman's home.

'Why not?' she asked herself. After

all, Miss Parkes had shown herself keen to know Ellie better. Without the presence of her cousins there to stifle what she might say, the thought of being free to have an open discussion, Ellie found strangely exciting. So, she reasoned, what if Miss Parkes had been a mistress of Mr Gerald Cookson, the younger, it was none of her concern. Ellie convinced her own mind that she cared not so long as she unearthed the truth and courted help with her dire situation. She would present herself there as a friend of Miss Parkes and then decide what she would say and do next, depending upon the reaction of the lady of the house. If she was turned away, it would make no difference to her current loathsome situation; she was a lost soul anyway. Ellie would try and find out something about the family of the Cooksons — one that she was a part of, although she had reason enough to question how at times, for she was treated with such indifference. She had enough experience of her aunt to know that Gertrude's cousin must be as easy to manipulate as anyone in the hall. Distantly, she must be related to the man she was supposed to marry. It did not feel right to her. It made no difference to her aunt, but Ellie was against this union for so many reasons that she would never go back to the hall. She would ask Miss Parkes for help and, if that request fell on uncaring ears, she would continue on her own way — she would find Mr Gerald Cookson junior, and would be bold enough to ask him outright for his help. She was certain he did not wish her to be married to his father, whatever the reason; his repugnance at the idea was true.

The lady, Miss Parkes, had revealed herself to be a free thinker. Surely she would not approve of a young woman being forced into a marriage which she wanted no part in. With this determined thought she marched stoically onwards. Ellie was about to revolt against her aunt's plans, which would place her in a situation that would never be forgiven.

Ellie felt that her confidence and resolve was draining away from her as her energy also sapped from her as she crossed the fields and started the walk up the long forested drive to the manor. She was near to exhaustion as she arrived at the large doors. Ellie was certain she must look a sight of flustered dishevelment. Still, she boldly walked up the steps to the main entrance and lifted the heavy door knocker, which was shaped like the head of an eagle. After what seemed like an age, but was in fact no more than a few moments, the door was opened by a man dressed in a deep red livery.

He raised a surprised eyebrow as he stared at her. Ellie stood with her back straight and as much presence, as her aunt would say, as she could achieve.

'Yes, miss?' he said simply, and looked as if for a carriage or horse.

'Please inform your mistress that

Miss Ellie has called upon her and wishes to speak with her in private. Miss Ellie, her friend from the Old Hall.' She stood still as he paused for a moment.

'If you wait inside, miss. I shall not keep you waiting long.' He stepped aside so that she may enter the house that she had felt so comfortable in such a short time ago. Everything inside this vast renovated building was plastered and painted in fresh pastel shades of azure, primrose or the new Wedgewood blue, with white classical decor as a contrast. Where the old manor house had been allowed to decay by its former owner, it now stood proud and was obviously well loved. The Old Hall, by comparison, was dark and oppressive, stifling her spirit, whereas this magnificent manor was light, fresh and lacked the dark haunting shadows of past owners. They had been removed and the place filled with delicate or beautiful adornments. Here she wanted to smile and breathe freely.

So she waited, happily admiring every little detail of the delightful plasterwork which edged the entrance hall's ceiling. With her composure regained, she felt able to relax. This had the effect of making her want to yawn; a wave of exhaustion swept over her. If only, she thought, I could stay in such a place.

'Ellie!' Miss Parkes almost ran to meet her as she appeared from a doorway of a room further along the hall. She was undoing an apron, which appeared to have paint colours smudged upon it. Miss Parkes pulled at its straps as she gave up trying to undo the bow at her back and pulled it over her head. Tossing it casually to her liveried footman, she continued to greet Ellie with an open embrace not bothering about the loose hair that now surrounded her face.

'Judd, ask Mrs Hobson to organise a tray for us. Fresh lemon juice and some toast and honey I think. A snack like that always sets me up for the day.' She took a step back from a speechless Ellie.

She hardly seemed to notice Ellie's inability to respond to the gesture. She carried on by taking Ellie's hands in hers and smiled straight at her. 'Tell me, my young friend, what amazing set of circumstances has allowed the quiet Ellie to arrive at my door unannounced. Something major, disturbing, or annoying at the very least, I should wager. Not trouble I hope?' She stared into Ellie's hesitant eyes as they began to well up with unshed tears.

She could not help herself. Ellie did not dare utter a word as she was becoming uncontrollably emotional. How long it had been that she had wanted someone to give her such a warm, caring and genuine welcome as this. Yet the woman was almost a complete stranger to her. She swallowed and pulled her hands away from those of her host. 'I'm sorry, forgive my appalling manners. I should not have come here. My problems are not yours nor should they be. I must find my own solution. I must go away and find help. I apologise. Please do not inform my aunt that I have been here. It is best she has no knowledge of my whereabouts. Just pretend I never arrived. I was walking and presumed to . . . I . . . '

She was led like a child back into the room that Miss Parkes had just left. The room had large windows, opposite which a canvas was propped upon an easel.

'You are not going anywhere, my little friend, until I know what has put you in such a state of confusion. Take off your coat and hat and sit down, please. Refreshments will arrive in a minute and then I want to hear what troubles you because, Ellie, I am about to make your troubles into my own. Two heads are better than one, particularly when both are female.' Miss Parkes laughed at her own quip but Ellie froze.

Ellie was staring at the painting

without removing any of her outer garments. Upon it was a portrait, as yet incomplete. It was of a man, a handsome man, and Ellie recognised the eyes of the not yet painted face. The eyes of Mr Gerald Cookson the younger, stared back at her. They were so telling, so bold, so enticing and so revealing. It must be true, she thought. This lady — this gifted lady, was painting her lover and she had interrupted her private time as she prepared this work — a special work of love, possibly a gift just for him, and Ellie had seen it first.

She had taken daring strides across the open countryside until she had stepped foot on the well tended lands of the immaculately kept Penny Manor. Now inside her, her heart was finally breaking, as she looked into the eyes of this man, remembering his touch. Wondering if her new friend felt the same each time he touched her in the intimacy of her own, marvellous home, and a strange yearning replaced the feelings of exhaustion that had threatened to overwhelm her.

'Ellie . . . Ellie are you all right?' Miss Parkes' voice trickled through to her barely conscious state as she seated herself on the edge of the window seat.

'Yes . . . But I must leave now. I am intruding on your time and your moments of . . . I understand now. I have proven myself to be no more than a foolish maid. I will . . . '

'Ellie, what do you mean?' Miss Parkes looked at her own painting, thoughtfully, then stared at Ellie and smiled. 'My dear Ellie, you have fallen for Gerry and his charms, haven't you?' She laughed, then put a hand over her mouth, delicately, as Ellie was about to stand up again. The servant returned with a tray and Miss Parkes' composure returned to her until he left. Then she put a hand out to Ellie. 'Listen, I don't know what has passed between you and Gerald, or what you presume has been happening between me and my good friend, but I fear you are misguided.

Gerald asked for a portrait to be completed for his new rooms in London. He is going to use it as an introduction of my work to his clients and the city, should they comment upon it. Meanwhile, he will have a portrait to hang of himself looking very grand and austere, which will impress his clientele, without incurring the costs of London's finest artists. Do you think I am doing this only for my own satisfaction and pleasure? I paint to make extra money and because I love to. I love the process of painting, Ellie, not the subject within it.'

Ellie nodded. 'They said that you and he were . . . '

Miss Parkes' cheeks flushed deeply. 'I do not care what 'they' say for 'they' are so often wrong!'

'I am sorry. I am so confused. I know I hardly know the man, but I would change that, Miss Parkes; I have watched him at the hall. He has spoken to me earnestly and . . . well, we seem to have an understanding between us. I am not at liberty to know him better because my aunt would force me to marry her cousin, his father. Then it will be too late and I have no way of escaping this union unless I run away. They also say that he,' she pointed to the portrait, 'is a cad and abuser of young maids, but I don't see him like that. I think he is a gentle lost soul also.'

'Stop, Ellie, give your brain a rest. You have been placed in an impossible situation, my dear. I can see that. Now you must eat and drink. Rest your feet, kick off those boots and I shall have them cleaned for you. Stay here with me. I will have a room and a hot tub made ready for you. You are going to be my guest, I insist. I will send word that I have invited you and that you are safe and well. Let your aunt dare to challenge that! I invite you to stay with me until we have sorted your pretty mess out. This is not the Middle Ages, we shall not have a woman forced into a loveless match. But if I know Gerry at all, and believe me I know him well enough, for he acted as my lawyer when I was living in London and Mama's estate became my own. You may yet have a knight on a charger to interject on your behalf. I think you need some time alone or at least alone with me.' She smiled. 'That is before you decide what you want from your life and who you want to share it with. Gerry is a dear friend of mine. He is no saint, but neither would he abuse a young maid. He would take advantage of those who offer him their attentions freely in a mature relationship, but not in the way those witches would have you believe. However, what concerns me more is this marriage you speak of to his father. It is the first I have heard of it. Very odd! You must eat and relax, and then you can tell me about this proposed marriage because I do not believe you should marry any man against your wishes.' She leaned back into her chair, tucking up her feet under her skirts.

'But I have no money of my own and nowhere else to live, so I must do as

Aunt Gertrude wishes.'

'Poppycock! You must not do any such thing, because here in Penny Manor I have fifteen bedrooms and more money than I can think of ever needing. So, my friend, if I give my patronage to you, you can make your own mind up about what you wish to do in life, can't you?'

Ellie stared, bewildered. She was being offered a home, help and a way out from under Gertrude's control. She ate the toast and drank the warm fluid. 'Thank you,' she uttered the words not knowing what else to say; the words seemed inadequate to the gratitude she felt, but they would have to suffice for now, because Ellie could not take in the enormity of what the woman suggested. Freedom, with no apparent cost attached.

* * *

Gerald saw the coach in the town stabled behind the inn. Samuel was busy inside the building. It did not take long for Gerald to ascertain that his father was not in his offices. He approached the ostler man with a jar of porter.

'Samuel, where is your mistress?' He perched himself on a three legged stool on the other side of a table to where Samuel was busy drinking and fondling the barmaid whose bosoms were spilling out of the neckline of her stained blouse.

'At your father's house, sir,' the man drawled.

'Why are you here, Samuel? You are in no fit state to drive the coach like that.'

'Ain't goin' anywhere for a while, am I Peg?' He nuzzled the wench's neck. She smiled but her eyes remained hard as the life she led. 'Don't worry, sir. Your pa gave me coin to come and wet me whistle.'

Gerald, on hearing this, raised both eyebrows. 'You best stay here then,' he added before leaving him with the jug of porter. He tied his horse to the back of the coach and climbed up on the carriage, releasing the brake. Samuel could find his own way back. If he chose to be drunk in the middle of the afternoon and waste good coin on a whore, then he would sober up on the walk back to the Old Hall.

9

The doors to his father's home were apparently unattended as Gerald stopped the carriage outside the front of the large country house. Gerald saw no reason to slam on the knocker and have a servant announce his arrival, so he secured the vehicle and let himself in.

He paused inside the hall to see if anyone stirred to greet him. As he heard voices coming from the morning room, he walked slowly over to the doorway, staying slightly out of sight. Realising it was his grandmother's voice he heard regaling someone with the benefit of her wisdom upon the virtues of being a devoted and obedient wife, he listened carefully to hear the response from the poor soul who had to endure her words. The voice that commented and agreed upon her advice was obviously that of

Cybil. Relieved that it was not the voice of Ellie, Gerald walked over to his father's study and boldly entered. It was empty. He then checked the library to no avail and so returned to the entrance hall. Taking two steps at a time, Gerald made his way quietly up the stairs to the first landing. Here he saw a servant making her way quietly along the corridor and just about to slip down the servants' stairs to the kitchen area below.

'Wait,' he said quietly.

The servant jumped nervously at the unexpected sound of his voice.

'Where is my father? He is usually at work in his office at this hour.'

The servant stepped uneasily aside.

'He is taking a rest and is not to be disturbed, sir.' The young girl glanced awkwardly towards the door of the willow room. 'He left instruction that no one was to disturb him. Excuse me, for I should be still in the kitchens, sir. Can I fetch you anything, sir?'

He shook his head and gestured with

his hand that she was free to go and for that moment he stood still. Then almost in a haze of silence he walked towards the door of the bedchamber. Either the man was ill, or there was perhaps a less palatable reason why the man, his father, had taken abed when he had guests within his house.

He very carefully placed his hand upon the door knob and turned it so patiently, that it made no discernable noise as the door came free of its catch. He let it open but a few inches; enough for him to see the bed itself. As he suspected, two people lay entwined upon it. What he could not stomach was that his father was lying there embracing Gertrude Hemmings, his own cousin. He would have hoped his father had better taste for a finer woman. He could see why the beautiful maid, Ellie, would appeal to a man in his middle years and seeking to regain his youth, but to lie with Gertrude made no sense to him at all. Amelia had been a lady and his own dear mother before her had been one in every way. She had loved the man she married, but the man changed into a cold unfeeling patriarch once she died. Once her untimely death left him with an heir, he could not bear to have him in his house, as he looked so like her.

He left the door on its catch and walked back down the stairs, retracing his steps to the study. The old man had a reason for trapping the young woman, Ellie, into a marriage, Gerald was certain of it. His father was looking for something more than companionship and lost youth. He had money, position and loved attending his club. What was Gertrude to do with it? If he wanted the old harridan, why involve the girl at all? Much as Gerald had respected his father and all the man's achievements in life, he had turned his own father's failure in life — his legacy after a spell in a debtors' prison, into a successful family, looking after his mother who he cherished. He would not stand by and see him destroy any more beauty, if he loved the ugliness that was Gertrude Hemming; even if it cost their relationship and he found himself disinherited. He did not need the man's money, he would save Ellie.

Gerald burst into the study and started rummaging through the desk drawers. What he sought, he knew not. But once he found it, he would ride to the Old Hall and release the girl from her invisible chains. She had a life to live. He had sensed her spirit and felt her sumptuous body. The father would not have her, but Gerald reasoned as he searched the room, the son might.

The desk drawers held no answers. He felt behind the first drawer and triggered the small lever releasing the hidden panel his father had had installed underneath the top of the desk. There the paper was revealed and slid forward still in its leather wrapping.

He sat back in the large leather chair and untied the thong which secured them. Carefully he straightened out the document which was inside, and highly decorated. It was, he could clearly see, a will — a legacy for Mademoiselle Eléanor Aveline Jacques.

'She is French!' he whispered.

Reading the detail of the document he clearly understood why Ellie — Miss Eléanor had been secreted away from the greater world and why Gertrude was so eager for this marriage to go ahead.

He secured the paper again and slipped it into his inside pocket, taking care to replace the secret drawer in the desk as if it had never been disturbed.

He then took a deep breath, releasing the air slowly as he thought for a moment. He could face his father here and now, but no, this was too risky. The old man was about to commit an immoral act and with, it appeared, no conscience. Therefore he was no longer a man he could predict the actions of. He would release the girl and explain things to her. Then escort her to London where he could secure her future. This piece of paper was going to change things considerably.

Gerald left the study and walked toward the door as his father appeared at the top of the flight of stairs.

'Gerald, good to see you.' He moved nimbly down the stairs for a man of his age. He looked slightly flushed in his usual ruddy cheeks, but was his normal confident self.

'I just came in to ask you a question, Father.' Gerald watched him walk toward him, steady, staring him eye to eye. No hint of guilt or remorse. His shoulders straight and his head held high.

'What would that be?' he smiled, welcoming. 'We could go into my study and share a glass of port or sherry.' He made his offer and gestured towards the room.

'We could, Father, but I would rather not.'

'You are in a hurry? Why come by at all, if you can not spare your father a few moments of your time?' his father said sternly.

'I wish to know, sir, if it is true that you are intending to marry a young woman called Ellie, who is younger than your own son.' He stared as his father looked impassively at him.

He shrugged his shoulders. 'Would that offend you, Gerald? We can talk in my study, not here where the servants can listen or my guests, Gertrude and Cybil. I was just making sure that Gertie is woken as she needed to rest after her journey.'

Gerald did not move.

'Many a man would willingly marry such a wench. I am not getting any younger, son. I need someone to look after me and be my companion, as I move toward my dotage. Surely, you would not begrudge your father that?' The man was trying to look sincere. But if Gerald had not doubted before, he certainly would have now. His father was far from his dotage, at least in his own opinion.

'You choose this girl for no other reason?' he asked.

'Why else? Of course this is the reason. What else? She is a poor orphan who Gertrude has kindly reared. I know that she is able and I can provide her with this magnificent town house, and soon, perhaps, a home in Harrogate too. You know I want to move my practice there. Mother is not very able these days and needs companionship; whilst I am busy, the girl can see to her needs.'

'Reared?' Gerald felt his stomach knot. This man had lied to him face to face. He cared nothing for Ellie, only what was written on the paper that Gerald had now protected in a pocket next to his heart. He would definitely save her from this man he realised he hardly knew.

'I must leave. I bid you good day, sir.' Gerald opened the door wide letting a gust of fresh air sweep into the hall.

'Won't you wish me luck?' his father asked.

Gerald glanced back as he left, but could not answer the man with honesty or integrity. Instead, he walked to the back of the carriage, untied his horse, mounted the animal and galloped off down the drive.

★ ★ ★

A few moments passed as the older man watched his son leave the estate. He wondered if he had any notion of the man he had become. There was a time he had held his first born son in his arms and a tear had rimmed his eyes. Then he had a beautiful and gentle woman as a wife. He had almost loved her. Her father had been rich and astute. He had granted the wedding and they had enjoyed the benefit of her dowry, but the father had insisted that she maintain some her family's estate, when the time came for it to pass to their only daughter, for her children. So he had never managed to hold onto the vast fortune that his arrogant son had benefited from. Even the years with Gertrude had not broken the lad's spirit, which he begrudgingly had to admire. Now he rode around the country as if he was the master of all he surveyed. No need to inherit again then. What he was about to do, Gerald senior, told himself, was for the good of young Thomas, who would have a young mother and her wealth.

Gertrude walked up behind him. 'Who was that?' she asked, as she put the last wisp of a straying hair back under her bonnet.

'It was young Gerald, Gertie. I fear his pride has been badly dented. He does not like to think of me remarrying without consulting him first. All these years and he has not forgiven me for turning him out of his home after his mother left us. Do not worry. He will return to London and in a couple of years, no doubt, he will speak to me again. It is his way.' He smiled at her, but she was looking toward the study. 'So while he is away we can be together as we should have been, once things have been taken care of. I do not care for silly young girls.'

'You must at least for a month or two. Then once you move away, she can stay with your mother here whilst we live in Harrogate. Oh, it will be a dream come true,' she whispered. 'Of course we shall have to wait for my girls to move out first.' She looked back towards his study. 'Gerald, we should check your study. Something is not right, my dear.'

'You worry too much, my love,' he whispered back to her, and closed the door. 'However, if it will put your mind at rest, my dear, then come and look upon our future security one last time.' He smiled at her, but she did not reply with a similar gesture.

'If I worry too much, then why is there a muddy footprint leading directly into your study?'

10

Ellie ate and talked to her new friend, telling her what little she knew about her parents, her life at the hall, and the scant plans for her future. She was also honest about how confusing her emotions were when it came to her suitor's elder son. When Miss Parkes announced she had heard quite enough she stood up and suggested that she rest whilst a bath was filled for her so that she could refresh herself.

Ellie was shown to a room by a servant. It was bigger than Gertude's main bedchamber. Light and beautiful, it was like no other she had ever seen other than the one in her dream. For in the hand-painted paper which decorated the walls was a little bird which sat upon a twisted vine, a complex pattern of flora and fauna that ran from top to the bottom of each piece.

However, the bird had been added. It was intricate and delicate. The small bird reminded her of the child's slippers and the edging on the pillow cover which haunted her sleep. When Miss Parkes entered the room, it was not the window that she gazed out of but the little bird she stared at, taking in the detail of the feathering which was painted so carefully, to make it as lifelike as the artist possibly could.

'The design is from 'The tree of life'. I decided to extract the bird and paint it for my own enjoyment. Do you approve?' She came into the room and seated herself on the window-seat overlooking the vast grounds.

'Yes, it is beautiful, but it is very similar to one that I see in my dreams.' She blushed slightly.

'You must have beautiful dreams then. Unlike the nightmare you have lived. Tell me, have you never met Gerald's father?'

'No, I have never seen him. I cannot imagine why he would want to make an offer of marriage to a stranger who has so little, Miss Parkes,' she said, as she turned to look at her new friend.

'Oh, I can think of one reason, Ellie: your beauty.'

Ellie blushed and laughed. 'My aunt is always telling me that I am ungainly, that my hair is a mess and that I am by nature plain in features. She does not approve of vanity and staring into a looking glass.'

'Do you never look at your own reflection?'

Ellie shook her head.

Miss Parkes stood up, took hold of Ellie's hand and led her into another room which adjoined the one Ellie had been in. There a hot bath had been prepared for her. One wall had a full length mirror fastened to it.

'I shall leave you to wash. Never be afraid of your own reflection, Ellie. When you can face yourself in a mirror for what you truly are, then you can face the world with confidence. You relax and take a moment to look at yourself and be honest about what you see, admitting in your heart that you are a beautiful woman who will turn many a man's head, if you are given the chance. I will lay out a day dress on the bed for you to change into. There are towels there. Come down to the conservatory when you are ready. Then we shall plan what we shall do next to help you begin life anew. There are so many things I would like you to see. I suggest we pack and leave for the city — London. But first, I will send word to Gerald to come here; we may yet need a man's advice on this repugnant affair.'

She left Ellie alone staring at her bedraggled appearance. She unpinned her hair and let it hang loose. The blonde curls cascaded over her shoulder. She enjoyed the sensation, knowing how her aunt would have called her a hussy, or worse. She turned and looked at her reflection in the mirror. The woman she saw was cowed, her shoulders sagged and rounded, her eyes dulled by years of being made to feel shame for being what she was: the daughter of whom? A woman, obviously, but what type of woman? Then, as if in a trance, she held her shoulders back, straightened her spine, undid the small buttons that fastened the front of her dress over her breasts, and then let the dress fall to the ground. As her undergarments were also released from their fastenings, she looked up at her own nakedness and stood proud with moist eyes. She was far from ugly, she was beautiful. Ellie slipped into the warmth of the water and let it envelop her body, caressing it, as she submerged under the rose petals which had been scattered on the surface. Ellie knew that this bath symbolised more than cleanliness. She would step out of it with a refreshed body and a renewed and more confident spirit.

★ ★ ★

The secret panel of the desk was released and the empty space revealed within. Mr Cookson sat back on the chair as he stared, first in disbelief that his son could have been so cunning, and then with great concern as he saw the expression bordering grief and panic on Gertude's face.

'Is it there?' she asked in a desperate hope that she was reading his face wrongly.

'He must have it, Gertie.' He closed the desk.

'Then I will send Samuel to apprehend him.' She walked to the door.

'No, he is in Gorebeck and it will do no good. Gerald is a man of the law. If he has the will then he knows the truth of it. We have been found out, Gertie. The little bird will be given her wings.' He stood up and walked over to her.

'No, he will want her fortune for himself. He will take her to London and flatter her. Before the stupid child knows what he is about he will have a special licence and he will inherit her fortune. It is no more than a month to her twenty-first birthday when her family estate is entrusted to her, or her husband. Gerald it should be you — not he. Stop him! How will we ever be free now — our home in Harrogate, and the house in London, we had such plans, Gerry.' She leaned her head upon his chest.

'We will just have to wait a little longer. I will find a companion for mother and then once your girls have married, we shall see.'

'I won't have it,' she snapped.

'You have no choice, Gertie. Not this time.'

'But . . . I want . . . '

'No, Gertie, all is lost, for now.' She collapsed into the chair by the fire, sobbing tears of frustration and fury as he took the key from his chain and opened the cupboard where he kept his best port, wondering if this time he had finally lost the respect of his eldest son. He felt surprisingly sad, not because he had let Gertie's plan fail, but because he realised how much he did love his eldest son.

* ★ ★

Gerald rode toward the hall, but as he left the town behind and headed for the open road he met Jackson, the groom from Penny Manor.

'Sir, I was sent for you. Miss Parkes asks that you call urgently. She says to tell you that a mutual friend is in need of your professional help.'

'A mutual friend?' he repeated.

'A lady,' he added.

Gerald galloped for the manor. He knew only one lady who was in trouble and if she had made it to Penny Manor then she was at least safe.

He dismounted before the horse came to a stop and flung the manor doors open wide.

'Gerald, you know how to make an entrance, dear,' Miss Parkes said, as she had just descended the stairs.

'Lizzie, where is Miss Eléanor — Ellie?'

he asked, hardly taking a breath.

'She is in the main guest room. I need to talk to you; the girl is in trouble and . . . '

She watched him bound up the stairs and disappear along the landing. She grinned, adding to herself, 'She may yet be in the bath.'

Gerald did not hear her words. He knocked lightly on the room door for he knew it well having stayed there on several occasions. Lizzie and he had known each other since he rented rooms in her brother's house when he was at Cambridge. He presumed Ellie was resting as he opened the door and walked straight in. First he saw the pale lemon day dress on the bed. He stared for a moment, and then turned; a scent of rose petals drifted into the room as Ellie emerged from the adjoining room wrapped in a large white towel.

He stared at her, from golden hair to naked toes, taking in every curve in between; the flush of colour showing in her cheek adding to the overall delightful effect upon his senses.

'I make no apology for being so keen to see you again, Ellie, for I bring you the most excellent news.' He smiled and then closed the door to the room.

He put his hand in his pocket and pulled out the documents he had stolen away from his father's desk.

'What are they?' she asked, as she walked barefoot to the edge of the bed, looking at the leather wrapped parchment. She noticed an embossed seal upon the back featuring a little bird; the same little bird that appeared in her dreams.

'These tell us who you really are. Sit down next to me and I will explain.'

Holding the towel close to her body she sat down.

'Eléanor — that is your name — Mademoiselle Eléanor Aveline Jacques. You are from an old and wealthy family in France. I am sad to say that your parents are dead, your father due to the troubles and your mother, I understand from an accompanying letter, was spared by virtue of her escape with an English officer, Gertrude's brother Bertram. She died in London and is buried there. He had you whisked away to England, because the fortune that the woman left was not given to Bertam as they never married; instead, she willed it all to you on your twenty-first year, or to your husband if you are wed. I am ashamed to say that my father and his cousin planned to keep your identity away from you. You would have been married, they would have their hands on your fortune and you, dear Ellie, would be left looking after my old grandmother who rambles ceaselessly in her own world. He never wanted a young wife; he wanted the legacy — your legacy.'

'The nightmare! The child within it was me? I was abducted!'

He nodded.

'I am rich?'

He nodded again.

'I do not need to marry if I do not choose to.'

He shrugged.

She smiled, her eyes filled with life, the dullness washed away.

'Why, though, the little bird in my dream?' she asked, as she stood to face him.

'Aveline is the family name passed down; originally Germanic, it means 'little bird'.'

'Thank you,' she said, and leaned over to kiss his cheek. His arms encircled her body and guided her to him. She felt his strength and his need as they kissed unashamedly and freely. She responded, wrapping her arms around his neck. He stood to his full height, lifting her in his arms as the towel slipped to her waist. She gasped, but he bent low and pulled up the fabric letting his hand brush against the soft flesh as he repaired her modesty. She watched his eyes; the desire in them matched her own as they held each other tightly, and she felt the palm of his hand resting against her breast, only the towel separating them.

He swallowed. 'I do not want your money, Ellie, but I would like to know you . . . better. You are free to choose any man you wish now, or not. You have that choice also. I am not my father.' He flushed, and his hands dropped to his side.

'I may not wish to marry just yet, but I at last know who I am and what I want. Perhaps we could share my journey, if you have patience?' She looked into his deep brown eyes and saw an almost imperceptible nod, as she placed her hand upon his and drew him back to her.

She had emerged as a beautiful woman, a little bird free to fly at last — but not alone anymore.

THE END

CHLOE'S FRIEND
A PHOENIX RISES
ABIGAIL MOOR:
THE DARKEST DAWN

We do hope that you have enjoyed reading this large print book.

Did you know that all of our titles are available for purchase?

We publish a wide range of high quality large print books including:
Romances, Mysteries, Classics
General Fiction
Non Fiction and Westerns

Special interest titles available in large print are:
The Little Oxford Dictionary
Music Book, Song Book
Hymn Book, Service Book

Also available from us courtesy of Oxford University Press:
Young Readers' Dictionary
(large print edition)
Young Readers' Thesaurus
(large print edition)

For further information or a free brochure, please contact us at:
Ulverscroft Large Print Books Ltd.,
The Green, Bradgate Road, Anstey,
Leicester, LE7 7FU, England.
Tel: (00 44) **0116 236 4325**
Fax: (00 44) **0116 234 0205**

Other titles in the
Linford Romance Library:

CHRISTMAS AT
HARTFORD HALL

Fenella Miller

When Elizabeth's grandfather died, there was no sign of a will; and, devastatingly, she discovered she was now dependent on his heir. When the new Lord and Lady Hartford and their twin daughters arrived, they reduced her status to that of a servant. Elizabeth is determined to leave Hartford Hall in the New Year and find work as a governess. But the arrival of Sir James Worthington to make an offer for Lady Eleanor only adds to her difficulties . . .

ABIGAIL MOOR: THE DARKEST DAWN

Valerie Holmes

Miss Abigail Hammond grows up in Beckton Manor as the adopted daughter of Lord Hammond. However, when he falls terminally ill, her life, her identity and her safety are all threatened. Then, faced with being forced into a marriage to a man she loathes, she runs away with her maid on Lord Hammond's instructions. Abigail tries to discover the truth of her past, despite her efforts being constantly foiled by her life-long maid, Martha.

STRANGERS IN THE NIGHT

Beth James

The man of her dreams sweeps Dee into a romantic last dance at her friend's wedding — then promptly disappears. When they meet again, it's in unpleasant circumstances. She finds that they are on opposite sides in a conflict that involves a promise Dee made to her favourite aunt. There is no way to resolve the situation — Dee cannot compromise, yet her heart tells her that Jack is the man for her. Sometimes however, love will find a way . . .